CRITICAL MASS
Includes the Hugo Award-Winning Short Story, "THE MEETING"

The inhabitants of the future are modern in every respect. They're synthesized. Specialized. And mechanized. Even the robot taxis argue the outcome of the All-Star games. They know it all.

And yet—
Who could guess that interstellar symbiants had infringed on the ecosphere? Or that the Holocaust had been prefigured in a macrocosmic math? Or that the fate of the children's army would depend on the damaged psyche of a single man?

In
CRITICAL MASS
Frederik Pohl and C. M. Kornbluth
Tales of a Future which could be Now

Bantam Science Fiction
Ask your bookseller for the books you have missed

ALAS, BABYLON by Pat Frank
A CANTICLE FOR LEIBOWITZ
    by Walter M. Miller, Jr.
CINNABAR by Edward Bryant
CRITICAL MASS by Frederik Pohl and
    C. M. Kornbluth
THE DAY OF THE DRONES by A. M. Lighter
THE DAY THE GODS DIED by Walter Ernsting
DHALGREN by Samuel R. Delany
DRAGONSONG by Anne McCaffrey
THE EMBEDDING by Ian Watson
FANTASTIC VOYAGE by Isaac Asimov
GLADIATOR-AT-LAW
    by Frederik Pohl and C. M. Kornbluth
HELLSTROM'S HIVE by Frank Herbert
THE HEPHAESTUS PLAGUE by Thomas Page
HIGH COUCH OF SILISTRA by Janet E. Morris
IN THE PROBLEM PIT by Frederik Pohl
KAMPUS by James E. Gunn
LOGAN'S RUN
    by William F. Nolan and
        George Clayton Johnson
MAN PLUS by Frederik Pohl
A MAZE OF DEATH by Philip K. Dick
THE MYSTERIOUS ISLAND by Jules Verne
NOVA by Samuel R. Delany
THE POWER OF THE SERPENT
    by Peter Valentine Timlett
THE SEEDBEARERS by Peter Valentine Timlett
SEARCH THE SKY
    by Frederik Pohl and C. M. Kornbluth
STAR OF THE UNBORN by Franz Werfel
TALES FROM THE CRYPT by Jack Olek
THE THREE STIGMATA OF PALMER ELDRITCH
    by Philip K. Dick
THE TIME MACHINE by H. G. Wells
THE TOWERS OF UTOPIA by Mack Reynolds
TRITON by Samuel R. Delany
TWILIGHT OF THE SERPENT
    by Peter Valentine Timlett
20,000 LEAGUES UNDER THE SEA by Jules Verne
UBIK by Philip K. Dick

Critical Mass

Frederik Pohl and C.M. Kornbluth

BANTAM BOOKS · TORONTO · LONDON · NEW YORK

RLI: $\dfrac{\text{VLM 8 (VLR 7–10)}}{\text{IL 9+}}$

CRITICAL MASS
A Bantam Book / October 1977

*Bantam Books are published by Bantam Books, Inc. Its trade-
mark, consisting of the words "Bantam Books" and the por-
trayal of a bantam, is registered in the United States Patent
Office and in other countries. Marca Registrada. Bantam
Books, Inc., 666 Fifth Avenue, New York, New York 10019.*

PRINTED IN THE UNITED STATES OF AMERICA

Contents

INTRODUCTION by Frederik Pohl   vii
THE QUAKER CANNON   1
MUTE INGLORIOUS TAM   31
THE WORLD OF MYRION FLOWERS   45
THE GIFT OF GARIGOLLI   53
A GENTLE DYING   83
A HINT OF HENBANE   93
THE MEETING   101
THE ENGINEER   117
NIGHTMARE WITH ZEPPELINS   127
CRITICAL MASS   137
AFTERWORD by Frederik Pohl   179

INTRODUCTION
by Frederik Pohl

During World War II I was an Air Force weatherman, mostly in Italy. My friend and collaborator Cyril Kornbluth had a varied career. He started out as a machinist with the artillery, a safe and reasonably satisfying job, as well as one pretty useful to the war effort. Along came ASTP. ASTP was a marvelously do-gooding program whereby certain soldiers could effectively drop out of the war entirely, attending college in uniform instead of fighting or holding down posts in the United States. I have never really understood what it had to do with the job of defeating Germany, Italy and Japan, but it surely was a dream of delight to every GI, and Cyril signed up for it at once.

Catch-22 came along in 1944. The Army perceived that what it really needed was not so much well-rounded officer material as warm bodies to throw against the enemy. ASTP was canceled without warning, and everyone in it was immediately reassigned to the infantry, as a private. The rest of us in uniform—*even* the rest of us—could not help feeling some compassion. When I went overseas it was on a troop transport that had once been a fruit-company freighter, called the *Cristobal*. About a hundred of the troops on board were weathermen like myself. The other 1,800 were former ASTP students, now about to join the Fifth Army's infantry divisions at Cassino. Some of them were still in their teens. Some of them had not been in the Army more than a few weeks. And some never walked away from Cassino.

At about the same time, in a different troop transport headed for England, Cyril was in a very similar convoy. He became a heavy machine-gunner, fought through the Battle of the Bulge and received a Bronze Star therefore. At least on paper he did. He never got the medal itself from the Army. I, on the other hand, had been given one, but it had never been made official; so a year or two after the war I gave him mine.

We both survived the war and returned to civilian life around the end of 1945. I went into the advertising business for a time in New York. Cyril went to the University of Chicago on the GI Bill of Rights.

Old fellow-Futurian Richard Wilson was also in Chicago in those years, getting into news work with Trans-Radio Press wire service. He soon became head of their Chicago bureau, and recruited Cyril to work in the newsroom. When Dick moved on to higher things, first in the Washington bureau and then to the central headquarters office in New York, Cyril replaced him as Chicago bureau chief, quitting college to make time for that eighteen-hour-a-day job.

A few years of that turned out to be enough. In 1951 Cyril came east, determined to go back to writing science fiction.

I had just bought the house I still live in, thirteen ancient rooms on the Jersey shore, and Cyril and his pregnant wife came to stay with us while they sorted out their plans. I had begun a science-fiction novel about the future of the advertising business, and invited Cyril to collaborate on finishing it. It became the first bit of science fiction to be published under the joint by-line "by Frederik Pohl and C. M. Kornbluth" (all our previous collaborations had appeared under a variety of pseudonyms) when Horace Gold serialized it in *Galaxy,* under the title of *Gravy Planet.* We were delighted. Horace paid us $1,400 for it, which was about as much money as either of us had ever seen in one lump before. A while later we managed to get Ian Ballantine to bring it out in book form, and, actually, it hasn't really done badly at all: something over ten million copies, in something like forty languages, earning something like a hundred times the price we wrote it for, as of even date. The book title was *The Space Merchants*.

Over the next half-dozen years we wrote six other novels together, three which were science fiction—*Gladiator-at-Law, Search the Sky* and *Wolfbane*—and three which were not. *Presidential Year* was about, well, about a presidential year: about a man who sought the nomination, and what he had to go through to get nominated. It appeared in 1956 and was well enough received critically, but not very exciting in sales. We sold the film rights, but the movie was never made; and one of the many reasons why I wish Cyril were still alive is that I would like it if we could have revised and reissued it in the new post-Watergate political scene. *A Town Is Drowning* was a topical novel about a hurricane hitting the East Coast. A couple of them had, not long before. One of them had taken part of my roof off and another had flooded Cyril's upstate New York house out, and we viewed the novel as an attempt to get even with the elements. *Sorority House* was a semisexy ripoff novel published under a pseudonym to complete a contract Cyril had come to regret having made. All of these non-sf novels had things in them which I like and wish we had used in better books, but we didn't.

At the same time we were going on with our own individual writing.

Cyril's own novels—*Takeoff, Not This August* and *The Syndic*—were appearing and doing very well (not to mention the half-dozen or so other novels, not science fiction, rather like *Sorority House,* which were appearing as paperback originals under pen names). We were both doing about as well as we had any reason to expect. I remember having a cup of coffee with Cyril when he had just had an editorial in the New York *Daily News* plugging one of his books, and I had been mentioned by *Time* in connection with one of mine. This sort of mass-media publicity for science fiction was not common in the fifties, and we were agreeably expectant of great things. We undertook to check with each other six months later to see what they had done for us in sales. (As it turned out, nothing we could detect.)

There was a certain amount of mutual assistance between us even on some of the stories which did not appear as collaborations. I remember specifically Cyril bogging down on his novel *Takeoff,* which he had originally intended to call something like *The Martians Upstairs,* with actual Martians in it. This proved complex and difficult to write, and we spent one long night replotting it into the published form, omitting the Martians. And I remember showing him the rough draft of my novella *The Midas Plague,* and getting from him some first-rate ideas on plotting and bits of business.

I think if Cyril had lived he would have become one of the all-time greats of the field. He was just hitting his stride when his health began to falter.

Cyril had always been a little plumper than was strictly good for him. When the Army made him a machine-gunner, lugging a 50-calibre-heavy MG around the Ardennes forest, they shortened his life. Exertions damaged his heart, and in his midthirties his doctor told him that he had a clear choice. He could give up smoking, drinking, spices in his food, a lot of the food itself, irregular hours and excitement; or he could die of hypertension.

For a while Cyril tried doing what the doctor told him. He took his medicine: tranquilizers, mostly, the not-quite-perfected tranquilizers of the fifties, which had such side-effects as making him a little confused and a little intellectually sluggish. He followed his diet rigorously. He came out to visit us during that period, and my wife cooked salt-free meals and baked salt-free bread. We couldn't do much writing. He was not up to it. But I showed him a novel I was having problems with. He read the pages of the first draft and handed it back to me. "Needs salt," he said, and that was all.

So I suppose Cyril made his choice. In his place, I think I might have made the same one. He went back to coffee and cigarettes, gave up the medication, went back to writing, finished the revisions on *Wolfbane,* wrote two or three of his best novelettes, signed on as an editor for *The Magazine of Fantasy and Science Fiction* —his first experiment with editing, rather than writing, science fiction, and one which he enjoyed enormously. ... And then on a snowy March morning I had a phone call from Mary, his wife, to say that Cyril had shoveled out their driveway to free his car, run to catch a train and dropped dead on the station platform.

He left a bundle of incomplete manuscripts and fragments, some of which I was later able to revise and complete. Most of the stories in this volume came out of that bale of paper, and were published after his death.

THE QUAKER CANNON

This story is about 12,000 words long. I see by my notes that the fragment Cyril left incomplete amounted to only about 3,000 words, which means that 9,000 of the words in the story are mine. And yet, reading it over, I can find no major plot element and only a few incidents that I remember contributing to it. This explains why I have trouble when someone asks me how much each of us contributed to our collaborations, and why my usual answer is, "I don't know."

LIEUTENANT JOHN KRAMER did crossword puzzles during at least eighty per cent of his waking hours. His cubicle in Bachelor Officers Quarters was untidy; one wall was stacked solid with newspapers and magazines to which he subscribed for their puzzle pages. He meant, from week to week, to clean them out but somehow never found time. The ern, or erne, a sea eagle, soared vertically through his days and by night the ai, a three-toed sloth, crept horizontally. In edes, or Dutch communes, dyers retted ecru, quaffing ades by the tun and thought was postponed.

John Kramer was in disgrace and, at thirty-eight, well on his way to becoming the oldest first lieutenant in the North American (and Allied) Army. He had been captured in '82 as an aftermath of the confused fighting around Tsingtao. A few exquisitely unpleasant months passed and he then delivered three TV lectures for the yutes. In them he announced his total conversion to Neo-Utilitarianism, denounced the North American (and Allied) military command as a loathesome pack of war-waging, anti-utilitarian mad dogs, and personally admitted the waging of viral warfare against the United Utilitarian Republics.

The yutes, or Utilitarians, had been faithful to their principles. They had wanted Kramer only for what he could do for them, not for his own sweet self, and when they had got the juice out of him they exchanged him. In '83 he came out of his fog at Fort Bradley, Utah, to find himself being court-martialed.

He was found guilty as charged, and sentenced to a reprimand. The lightness of the sentence was something to be a little proud of, if not very much. It stood as a grudging tribute to the months he had held out against involutional melancholia in the yute Blank Tanks. For exchanged PW's, the severity of their courts-martial was in inverse proportion to the duration of their ordeal in Utilitarian hands. Soldiers who caved in after a couple of days of sense-starvation could look forward only to a firing squad. Presumably a returned soldier dogged (or rigid) enough to be driven into hopeless insanity without cooperating would have been honorably acquitted by his court, but such a case had not yet come up.

Kramer's "reprimand" was not the face-to-face bawling-out suggested to a civilian by the word. It was a short letter with numbered paragraphs which said (1) you are reprimanded, (2) a copy of this reprimand will be punched on your profile card. This tagged him forever as a foul ball, destined to spend the rest of his military life shuffling from one dreary assignment to another, without hope of promotion or reward.

He no longer cared. Or thought he did not; which came to the same thing.

He was not liked in the Officers Club. He was bad company. Young officers passing through Bradley on their way to glory might ask him, "What's it *really* like in a Blank Tank, Kramer?" But beyond answering, "You go nuts," what was there to talk about? Also he did not drink, because when he drank he went on to become drunk, and if he became drunk he would cry.

So he did a crossword puzzle in bed before breakfast, dressed, went to his office, signed papers, did puzzles until lunch, and so on until the last one in bed at night. Nominally he was Commanding Officer of the 561st Provisional Reception Battalion. Actually he was (with a few military overtones) the straw boss of a gang of clerks in uniform who saw to the arrival, bedding, feeding, equipping, inoculation and transfer to a training unit of one thousand scared kids per week.

On a drizzle-swept afternoon in the spring of '85 Kramer was sounding one of those military overtones. It was his appointed day for a "surprise" inspection of Company D of his battalion. Impeccable in dress blues, he was supposed to descend like a thunderbolt on this company or that, catching them all unaware, striding arrogantly down the barracks aisle between bunks, white-gloved and eagle-eyed for dust, maddened at the sight of disarray, vengeful against such contraband as playing cards or light reading matter. Kramer knew, quite well, that one of his orderly room clerks always telephoned the doomed company to warn that he was on his way. He did not particularly mind it. What he minded was unfair definitions of key words, and ridiculously variant spellings.

The permanent-party sergeant of D Company bawled "Tench-*hut!*" when Kramer snapped the door open and stepped crisply into the barracks. Kramer froze his face into its approved expression of controlled annoyance and opened his mouth to give the noncom his orders. But the sergeant had miscalculated. One of the scared kids was still frantically mopping the aisle.

Kramer halted. The kid spun around in horror, made some kind of attempt to present arms with the mop and failed. The mop shot from his soapy hands like a slung baseball bat, and its soggy gray head schlooped against the lieutenant's dress-blue chest.

The kid turned white and seemed about to faint on the damp board floor. The other kids waited to see him destroyed.

Kramer was mildly irritated. "At ease," he said. "Pick up that mop. Sergeant, confound it, next time they buzz you from the orderly room don't cut it so close."

The kids sighed perceptibly and glanced covertly at each other in the big bare room, beginning to suspect it might not be too bad after all. Lieutenant Kramer then resumed the expression of a nettled bird of prey and strode down the aisle. Long ago he had worked out a "random" selection of bunks for special attention and now followed it through habit. If he had thought about it any more, he would have supposed that it was still spy-proof; but every noncom in his cadre had long since discovered that Kramer stopped at either every second bunk on the right and every third on the left, or every third bunk on the right and every second on the left—depending on whether the day of the month was odd or even. This would not have worried Kramer if he had known it; but he never even noticed that the men beside the bunks he stopped at were always the best-shaved, best-policed and healthiest looking in each barracks.

Regardless, he delivered a certain quota of meaningless demerits which were gravely recorded by the sergeant. Of blue-eyed men on the left and brown-eyed men on the right (this, at least, had not been penetrated by the noncoms) he went on to ask their names and home towns. Before discovering crossword puzzles he had memorized atlases, and so he had something to say about every home town he had yet encountered. In this respect at least he considered himself an above-average officer, and indeed he was.

It wasn't the Old Army, not by a long shot, but when the draft age went down to fifteen some of the Old Army's little ways had to go. One experimental reception station in Virginia was trying out a Barracks Mother system. Kramer, thankful for small favors, was glad they hadn't put him on that project. Even here he was expected, at the end of the inspection, to call the "men" around him and ask if anything was bothering them. Something always was. Some gangling kid would scare up the nerve to ask, gee, lieutenant, I know what the Morale Officer said, but exactly *why* didn't we ever use the megaton-head missiles, and another would want to know how come Lunar Base was such a washout, tactically speaking, sir. And then he would have to rehearse the dry "recommended discussion themes" from the briefing books; and then, finally, one of them, nudged on by others, would pipe up, "Lieutenant, what's it *like* in the Blank Tanks?" And he would know that already, forty-eight hours after induction, the kids all knew about what Lieutenant John Kramer had done.

But today he was spared. When he was halfway through the rigmarole the barracks phone rang and the sergeant apologetically answered it.

He returned from his office-cubicle on the double, looking vaguely frightened. "Compliments of General Grote's secretary, sir, and will you please report to him at G-1 as soon as possible."

"Thank you, sergeant. Step outside with me a moment." Out on the duckboard walk, with the drizzle trickling down his neck, he asked: "Sergeant, who is General Grote?"

"Never heard of him, sir."

Neither had Lieutenant Kramer.

He hurried to Bachelor Officers Quarters to change his sullied blue jacket, not even pausing to glance at the puzzle page of the *Times*, which had arrived while he was at "work." Generals were special. He hurried out again into the drizzle.

Around him and unnoticed were the artifacts of an Army base at war. Sky-eye search radars popped from their silos to scan the horizons for a moment and then retreat, the burden of search taken up by the next in line. Helicopter sentries on guard duty prowled the barbed-wire perimeter of the camp. Fort Bradley was not all reception center. Above-ground were the barracks, warehouses and rail and highway termini for processing recruits—ninety thousand men and all their goods—but they were only the skin over the fort itself. They were, as the scared kids told each other in the dayrooms, naked to the air. If the yutes ever *did* spring a megaton attack, they would become a thin coating of charcoal on the parade ground, but they would not affect the operation of the *real* Fort Bradley a bit.

The *real* Fort Bradley was a hardened installation beneath meters of reinforced concrete, some miles of rambling warrens that held the North American (and Allied) Army's G-1. Its business was people: the past, present and future of every soul in the Army.

G-1 decided that a fifteen-year-old in Duluth was unlikely to succeed in civilian schools and drafted him. G-1 punched his Army tests and civilian records on cards, consulted its card-punched tables of military requirements and assigned him, perhaps, to Machinist Training rather than Telemetering School. G-1 yanked a platoon leader halfway around the world from Formosa and handed him a commando for a raid on the yutes' Polar Station Seven. G-1 put foulball Kramer at the "head" of the 561st PRB. G-1 promoted and allocated and staffed and rewarded and punished.

Foulball Kramer approached the guardbox at the elevators to the warrens and instinctively squared his shoulders and smoothed his tie.

General Grote, he thought. He hadn't *seen* a general officer since he'd been commissioned. Not close up.

Colonels and majors had court-martialed him. He didn't know who Grote was, whether he had one star or six, whether he was Assignment, Qualifications, Training, Evaluation, Psychological—or Disciplinary.

Military Police looked him over at the elevator head. They read him like a book. Kramer wore his record on his chest and sleeves. Dull gold bars spelled out the overseas months—for his age and arm, the Infantry, not enough. "Formosa," said a green ribbon, and "the storming of the beach" said a small bronze spearpoint on it. A brown ribbon told them "Chinese Mainland," and the stars on it meant that he had engaged in three of the five mainland campaigns—presumably Canton, Mukden and Tsingtao, since they were the first. After that, nothing. Especially not the purple ribbon that might indicate a wound serious enough to keep him out of further fighting.

The ribbons, his age and the fact that he was still a first lieutenant were grounds enough for the MP's to despise him. An officer of thirty-eight should be a captain at least. Many were majors and some were colonels. "You can go down, Lieutenant," they told the patent foulball, and he went down to the interminable concrete tunnels of G-1.

A display machine considered the name *General Grote* when he typed it on its keyboard, and told him with a map where the general was to be found. It was a longish walk through the tunnels. While he walked past banks of clicking card-sorters and their servants he pondered other information the machine had gratuitously supplied: GROTE, Lawrence W, Lt Gen, 0-459732, Unassigned.

It did not lessen any of Kramer's puzzles. A three-star general, then. He couldn't *possibly* have anything to do with disciplining a lousy first-john. Lieutenant generals ran Army Groups, gigantic ad hoc assemblages of up to a hundred divisions, complete with air forces, missile groups, amphibious assault teams, even carrier and missile-sub task forces. The fact of his rank indicated that, whoever he was, he was an immensely able and tenacious person. He had gone through at least a twenty-year threshing of the wheat from the chaff, all up the screening and evaluation boards from second lieutenant to, say, lieutenant colonel, and then the murderous grind of accelerated courses at Command and General Staff School, the fanatically rigid selection for the War College, an obstacle course designed not to train the substandard up to competence but to keep them out. It was just this side of impossible for a human being to become a lieutenant general. And yet a few human beings in every generation did bulldoze their way through that little gap between the impossible and the almost impossible.

And such a man was unassigned?

Kramer found the office at last. A motherly, but sharp-eyed, WAC major told him to go right in.

John Kramer studied his three-star general while going through the ancient rituals of reporting-as-ordered. General Grote was an old man, straight, spare, white-haired, tanned. He wore no overseas bars. On his chest were all the meritorious service ribbons his country could bestow, but none of the decorations of the combat soldier. This was explained by a modest sunburst centered over the ribbons. General Grote was, had always been, General Staff Corps. A desk man.

"Sit down, Lieutenant," Grote said, eyeing him casually. "You've never heard of me, I assume."

"I'm afraid not, sir."

"As I expected," said Grote complacently. "I'm not a dashing tank commander or one of those flying generals who leads his own raids. I'm one of the people who moves the dashing tank commanders and flying generals around the board like chess pieces. And now, confound it, I'm going to be a dashing combat leader at last. You may smoke if you like."

Kramer obediently lit up.

"Dan Medway," said the general, "wants me to start from scratch, build up a striking force and hit the Asian mainland across the Bering Strait."

Kramer was horrified twice—first by the reference to The Supreme Commander as "Dan" and second by the fact that he, a lieutenant, was being told about high strategy.

"Relax," the general said. "Why you're here, now. You're going to be my aide."

Kramer was horrified again. The general grinned.

"Your card popped out of the machinery," he said, and that was all there was to say about that, "and so you're going to be a highly privileged character and everybody will detest you. That's the way it is with aides. You'll know everything I know. And vice versa; that's the important part. You'll run errands for me, do investigations, serve as hatchet man, see that my pajamas are pressed without starch and make coffee the way I like it—coarse grind, brought to the boil for just a moment in an old-fashioned coffee pot. Actually what you'll do is what I want you to do from day to day. For these privileges you get to wear a blue fourragère around your left shoulder which marks you as a man not to be trifled with by colonels, brigadiers or MP's. That's the way it is with aides. And, I don't know if you have any outside interests, women or chess or drinking. The machinery didn't mention any. But you'll have to give them up if you do."

"Yes, sir," said Kramer. And it seemed wildly possible that he might never touch pencil to puzzle again. With something to *do*—

"We're Operation Ripsaw," said the general. "So far, that's me, Margaret out there in the office and you. In addition to other duties, you'll keep a diary of Ripsaw, by the way, and I want you to have a summary with you at all times in case I need it. Now call in Margaret, make a pot of coffee, there's a little stove thing in the washroom there, and I'll start putting together my general staff."

It started as small and as quietly as that.

ii

It was a week before Kramer got back to the 561st long enough to pick up his possessions, and then he left the stacks of *Timeses* and *Saturday Reviews* where they lay, puzzles and all. No time. The first person to hate him was Margaret, the motherly major. For all her rank over him, she was a secretary and he was an aide with a fourragère who had the general's willing ear. She began a policy of nonresistance that was noncooperation, too; she would not deliberately obstruct him, but she would allow him to poke through the files for ten minutes before volunteering the information that the folder he wanted was already on the general's desk. This interfered with the smooth performance of Kramer's duties, and of course the general spotted it at once.

"It's nothing," said Kramer when the general called him on it. "I don't like to say anything."

"Go on," General Grote urged. "You're not a soldier any more; you're a rat."

"I think I can handle it, sir."

The general motioned silently to the coffee pot and waited while Kramer fixed him a cup, two sugars, no cream. He said: "Tell me everything, always. All the dirty rumors about inefficiency and favoritism. Your suspicions and hunches. Anybody that gets in your way—or more important, in mine. In the underworld they shoot stool-pigeons, but here we give them blue cords for their shoulders. Do you understand?"

Kramer did. He did not ask the general to intercede with the motherly major, or transfer her; but he did handle it himself. He discovered it was very easy. He simply threatened to have her sent to Narvik.

With the others it was easier. Margaret had resented him because she was senior in Operation Ripsaw to him, but as the others were sucked in they found him there already. Instead of resentment, their attitude toward him was purely fear.

The next people to hate him were the aides of Grote's general staff because he was a wild card in the deck. The five members of the staff—Chief, Personnel, Intelligence, Plans & Training and Operations—proceeded with their orderly, systematic jobs day by day, building Ripsaw . . . until the inevitable moment when Kramer would breeze in with, "Fine job, but the general suggests—" and the unhorsing of many assumptions, and the undoing of many days' work. That was his job also. He was a bird of ill omen, a coiled snake in fair grass, a hired killer and a professional betrayer of confidences—though it was not long before there were no confidences to betray, except from an occasional young, new officer who hadn't learned his way around, and those not worth betraying. That, as the general had said, was the way it was with aides. Kramer wondered sometimes if he liked what he was doing, or liked himself for doing it. But he never carried the thought through. No time.

Troops completed basic training or were redeployed from rest areas and entrained, emplaned, embussed or embarked for the scattered staging areas of Ripsaw. Great forty-wheeled trucks bore nuclear cannon up the Alcan Highway at a snail's pace. Air groups and missile sections launched on training exercises over Canadian wasteland that closely resembled tundra, with grid maps that bore names like Maina Pylgin and Kamenskoe. Yet these were not Ripsaw, not yet, only the separate tools that Ripsaw would someday pick up and use.

Ripsaw itself moved to Wichita and a base of its own when its headquarters staff swelled to fifteen hundred men and women. Most of them hated Kramer.

It was never perfectly clear to Kramer what his boss had to do with the show. Kramer made his coffee, carried his briefcase, locked and unlocked his files, delivered to him those destructive tales and delivered for him those devastating suggestions, but never understood just why there had to be a Commanding General of Ripsaw.

The time they went to Washington to argue an allocation of seventy rather than sixty armored divisions for Ripsaw, for instance, General Grote just sat, smiled and smoked his pipe. It was his chief of staff, the young and brilliant major general Cartmill, who passionately argued the case before D. Beauregard Medway, though when Grote addressed his superior it still was as "Dan." (They did get the ten extra divisions, of course.)

Back in Wichita, it was Cartmill who toiled around the clock coordinating. A security lid was clamped down early in the game. The fifteen hundred men and women in the Wichita camp stayed in the Wichita camp. Commerce with the outside world, except via coded messages to other elements of Ripsaw, was a capital offense—as three privates learned the hard way. But through those coded channels Cartmill reached out to every area of the North American (and Allied) world. Personnel scoured the globe for human components that might be fitted into Ripsaw. Intelligence gathered information about that tract of Siberia which they were to invade, and the waters they were to cross. Plans & Training slaved at methods of effecting the crossing and invasion efficiently, with the least (or at any rate the optimum least, consistent with requirements of speed, security and so on) losses in men and materiel. Operations studied and restudied the various ways the crossing and invasion might go right or wrong, and how a good turn of fortune could be exploited, a bad turn minimized. General Cartmill was in constant touch with all of them, his fingers on every cord in the web. So was John Kramer.

Grote ambled about all this with an air of pleased surprise.

Kramer discovered one day that there had been books written about his boss—not best sellers with titles like *"Bloody Larry" Grote, Sword of Freedom,* but thick, gray mimeographed staff documents, in Chinese and Russian, for top-level circulation among yute commanders. He surprised Grote reading one of them —in Chinese.

The general was not embarrassed. "Just refreshing my memory of what the yutes think I'm like so I can cross them up by doing something different. Listen: 'Characteristic of this officer's philosophy of attack is varied tactics. Reference his lecture, *Lee's 1862 Campaigns,* delivered at Fort Leavenworth Command & General Staff School, attached. Opposing commanders should not expect a force under him to do the same—' Hmm. *Tsueng,* water radical. '—under him to press the advance the same way twice.' Now all I have to do is make sure we attack by the book, like Grant instead of Lee, slug it out without any brilliant variations. See how easy it is, John? How's the message center?"

Kramer had been snooping around the message center at Grote's request. It was a matter of feeding out cigarettes and smiles in return for an occasional incautious word or a hint; gumshoe work. The message center was an underground complex of encoders, decoders, transmitters, receivers and switchboards. It was staffed by a Signal Corps WAC battalion in three shifts around the clock. The girls were worked hard—though a battalion should have been enough for the job. Messages went from and to the message center linking the Wichita brain with those seventy divisions training now from Capetown to Manitoba, a carrier task force conducting exercises in the Antarctic, a fleet of landing craft growing every day on the Gulf of California. The average time-lag between receipt of messages and delivery to the Wichita personnel at destination was 12.25 minutes. The average number of erroneous transmissions detected per day was three. Both figures General Grote considered intolerable.

"It's Colonel Bucknell that's lousing it up, General. She's trying too hard. No give. Physical training twice a day, for instance, and a very hard policy on excuses. A stern attitude's filtered down from her to the detachments. Everybody's chewing out subordinates to keep themselves covered. The working girls call Bucknell 'the monster.' Their feeling is the Army's impossible to please, so what the hell."

"Relieve her," Grote said amiably. "Make her mess officer; Ripsaw chow's rotten anyway." He went back to his Chinese text.

And suddenly it all began to seem as if it really might someday rise and strike out across the Strait. From Lieutenant Kramer's Ripsaw Diary:

At AM staff meeting CG RIPSAW xmitted order CG NAAARMY designating RIPSAW D day 15 May 1986. Gen CARTMILL observed this date allowed 45 days to form troops in final staging areas assuming RIPSAW could be staged in 10 days. CG RIPSAW stated that a 10-day staging seemed feasible. Staff concurred. CG RIPSAW so ordered. At 1357 hours CG NAAARMY concurrence received.

They were on the way.

As the days grew shorter Grote seemed to have less and less to do, and curiously so did Kramer. He had not expected this. He had been aide-de-camp to the general for nearly a year now, and he fretted when he could find no fresh treason to bring to the general's ears. He redoubled his prowling tours of the kitchens, the BOQ, the motor pools, the message center, but not even the guard mounts or the shine on the shoes of the soldiers at Retreat parade was in any way at fault. Kramer could only imagine that he was missing things. It did not occur to him that, as at last they should be, the affairs of Ripsaw had gathered enough speed to keep them straight and clean, until the general called him in one night and ordered him to pack. Grote put on his spectacles and looked over them at Kramer. "D plus five," he said, "assuming all goes well, we're moving this headquarters to Kiska. I want you to take a look-see. Arrange a plane. You can leave tomorrow."

It was, Kramer realized that night as he undressed, Just Something to Do. Evidently the hard part of his job was at an end. It was now only a question of fighting the battle, and for that the field commanders were much more important than he. For the first time in many months he thought it would be nice to do a crossword puzzle, but instead fell asleep.

It was an hour before leaving the next day that Kramer met Ripsaw's "cover."

The "cover" was another lieutenant general, a bristling and wiry man named Clough, with a brilliant combat record staked out on his chest and sleeves for the world to read. Kramer came in when his buzzer sounded, made coffee for the two generals and was aware that Grote and Clough were old pals and that the Ripsaw general was kidding the pants off his guest.

"You always were a great admirer of Georgie Patton," Grote teased. "You should be glad to follow in his footsteps. Your operation will go down in history as big and important as his historic cross-Channel smash into Le Havre."

Kramer's thoughts were full of himself—he did not much like getting even so close to the yutes as Kiska, where he would be before the sun set that night —but his ears pricked up. He could not remember any cross-Channel smash into Le Havre. By Patton or anybody else.

"Just because I came to visit your show doesn't mean you have to rib me, Larry," Clough grumbled.

"But it's such a pleasure, Mick."

Clough opened his eyes wide and looked at Grote. "I've generaled against Novotny before. If you want to know what I think of him, I'll tell you."

Pause. Then Grote, gently: "Take it easy, Mick. Look at my boy there. See him quivering with curiosity?"

Kramer's back was turned. He hoped his blush would subside before he had to turn around with the coffee. It did not.

"Caught red-faced," Grote said happily, and winked at the other general. Clough looked stonily back. "Shall we put him out of his misery, Mick? Shall we fill him in on the big picture?"

"Might as well get it over with."

"I accept your gracious assent." Grote waved for Kramer to help himself to coffee and to sit down. Clearly he was unusually cheerful today, Kramer thought. Grote said: "Lieutenant Kramer, General Clough is the gun-captain of a Quaker cannon which covers Ripsaw. He looks like a cannon. He acts like a cannon. But he isn't loaded. Like his late idol George Patton at one point in his career, General Clough is the commander of a vast force which exists on paper and in radio transmissions alone."

Clough stirred uneasily, so Grote became more serious. "We're brainwashing Continental Defense Commissar Novotny by serving up to him his old enemy as the man he'll have to fight. The yute radio intercepts are getting a perfect picture of an assault on Polar Nine being prepared under old Mick here. That's what they'll prepare to counter, of course. Ripsaw will catch them flatfooted."

Clough stirred again but did not speak.

Grote grinned. "All right. We *hope*," he conceded. "But there's a lot of planning in this thing. Of course, it's a waste of the talent of a rather remarkably able general—" Clough gave him a lifted-eyebrow look— "but you've got to have a real man at the head of the fake army group or they won't believe it. Anyway, it worked with Patton and the Nazis. Some unkind people have suggested that Patton never did a better bit of work than sitting on his knapsack in England and letting his name be used."

"All full of beans with a combat command, aren't you?" Clough said sourly. "Wait'll the shooting starts."

"Ike never commanded a battalion before the day he invaded North Africa, Mick. He did all right."

"Ike wasn't up against Novotny," Clough said heavily. "I can talk better while I'm eating, Larry. Want to buy me a lunch?"

General Grote nodded. "Lieutenant, see what you can charm out of Colonel Bucknell for us to eat, will you? We'll have it sent in here, of course, and the best girls she's got to serve it." Then, unusually, he stood up and looked appraisingly at Kramer.

"Have a nice flight," he said.

iii

Kramer's blue fourragère won him cold handshakes but a seat at the first table in the Hq Officers Mess in Kiska. He didn't have quite enough appetite to appreciate it.

Approaching the island from the air had taken appetite away from him, as the GCA autocontroller rocked the plane in a carefully calculated zigzag in its approach. They were, Kramer discovered, under direct visual observation from any chance-met bird from yute eyries across the Strait until they got below five hundred feet. Sometimes the yutes sent over a flight of birds to knock down a transport. Hence the zigzags.

Captain Mabry, a dark, tall Georgian who had been designated to make the general's aide feel at home, noticed Kramer wasn't eating, pushed his own tray into the center strip and, as it sailed away, stood up. "Get it off the pad, shall we? Can't keep the Old Man waiting."

The captain took Mabry through clanging corridors to an elevator and then up to the eyrie. It was only a room. From it the spy-bird missiles—rockets, they were really, but the services like to think of them as having a punch, even though the punch was only a television camera—were controlled. To it the birds returned the pictures their eyes saw.

Brigadier Spiegelhauer shook Kramer's hand. "Make yourself at home, Lieutenant," he boomed. He was short and almost skeletally thin, but his voice was enormous. "Everything satisfactory for the general, I hope?"

"Why, yes, sir. I'm just looking around."

"Of course," Spiegelhauer shouted. "Care to monitor a ride?"

"Yes, sir." Mabry was looking at him with amusement, Kramer saw. Confound him, what right did *he* have to think Kramer was scared—even if he was? Not a physical fear; he was not insane. But . . . scared.

The service life of a spy-bird over yute territory was something under twenty minutes, by then the homing heads on the ground-to-air birds would have sniffed out its special fragrance and knocked it out. In that twenty-minute period it would see what it could see. Through its eyes the observers in the eyrie would learn just that much more about yute dispositions—so long as it remained in direct line-of-sight to the eyrie, so long as everything in its instrumentation worked, so long as yute jamming did not penetrate its microwave control.

Captain Mabry took Kramer's arm. "Take 'er off the pad," Mabry said negligently to the launch officer. He conducted Kramer to a pair of monitors and sat before them.

On both eight-inch screens the officers saw a diamond-sharp scan of the inside of a silo plug. There was no sound. The plug lifted off its lip without a whisper, dividing into two semicircles of steel. A two-inch circle of sky showed. Then, abruptly, the circle widened; the lip irised out and disappeared; the gray surrounded the screen and blanked it out, and then it was bright blue, and a curl of cirrocumulus in one quadrant of the screen.

Metro had promised no cloud over the tactical area, but there was cloud there. Captain Mabry frowned and tapped a tune on the buttons before him; the cirrocumulus disappeared and a line of gray-white appeared at an angle on the screen. "Horizon," said Mabry. "Labble to make you seasick, Lootenant." He tapped some more and the image righted itself. A faint yellowish stain, not bright against the bright cloud, curved up before them and burst into spidery black smoke. "Oh, they are *anxious*," said Mabry, sounding nettled. "General, weather has busted it again. Cain't see a thing."

Spiegelhauer bawled angrily, "I'm going to the weather station," and stamped out. Kramer knew what he was angry about. It was not the waste of a bird; it was that he had been made to lose face before the general's aide-de-camp. There would be a bad time for the Weather Officer because Kramer had been there that day.

The telemetering crew turned off their instruments. The whining eighteen-inch reel that was flinging tape across a row of fifteen magnetic heads, recording the picture the spy-bird took, slowed and droned and stopped. Out of instinct and habit Kramer pulled out his rough diary and jotted down *Brig. Spiegelhauer— Permits bad wea. sta. situation?* But it was little enough to have learned on a flight to Kiska, and everything else seemed going well.

Captain Mabry fetched over two mugs of hot cocoa. "Sorry," he said. "Cain't be helped, I guess."

Kramer put his notebook away and accepted the cocoa.

"Beats U-2in'," Mabry went on. "Course, you don't get to see as much of the country."

Kramer could not help a small, involuntary tremor. For just a moment there, looking out of the spy-bird's eyes, he had imagined himself actually in the air above

yute territory and conceived the possibility of being
shot down, parachuting, internment, the Blank Tanks,
"Yankee! Why not be good fellow? You *proud* you
murderer?"

"No," Kramer said, "you don't get to see as much
of the country." But he had already seen all the yute
country he ever wanted.

Kramer got back in the elevator and descended
rapidly, his mind full. Perhaps a psychopath, a hungry
cat or a child would have noticed that the ride downward lasted a second or two less than the ride up.
Kramer did not. If the sound echoing from the tunnel he
walked out into was a bit more clangorous than the one
he had entered from, he didn't notice that either.

Kramer's mind was occupied with the thought
that, all in all, he was pleased to find that he had approached this close to yute territory, and to yute Blank
Tanks, without feeling *particularly* afraid. Even though
he recognized that there was nothing to be afraid of,
since of course the yutes could not get hold of him
here.

Then he observed that the door Mabry opened for
him led to a chamber he knew he had never seen before.

They were standing on an approach stage and below them forty-foot rockets extended downward into
their pit. A gantry-bridge hung across space from the
stage to the nearest rocket, which lay open, showing
a clumsily padded compartment where there should
have been a warhead or an instrument capsule.

Kramer turned around and was not surprised to
find that Mabry was pointing a gun at him. He had almost expected it. He started to speak. But there was
someone else in the shadowed chamber, and the first he
knew of *that* was when the sap struck him just behind
the ear.

It was all coming true: "Yankee! Why not be
honest man? You *like* murder babies?" Kramer only

shook his head. He knew it did no good to answer. Three years before he had answered. He knew it also did no good to keep quiet; because he had done that too. What he knew most of all was that nothing was going to do him any good because the yutes had him now, and who would have thought Mabry would have been the one to do him in?

They did not beat him at this point, but then they did not need to. The nose capsule Mabry had thrust him into had never been designed for carrying passengers. With ingenuity Kramer could only guess at Mabry had contrived to fit it with parachutes and watertight seals and flares so the yute gunboat could find it in the water and pull out their captive alive. But he had taken 15- and 20-G accelerations, however briefly. He seemed to have no serious broken bones, but he was bruised all over. Secretly he found that almost amusing. In the preliminary softening up, the yutes did not expect their captives to be in physical pain. By being in pain he was in some measure upsetting their schedule. It was not much of a victory but it was all he had.

Phase Two was direct questioning: What was Ripsaw exactly? How many divisions? Where located? Why had Lieutenant-General Grote spent so much time with Lieutenant-General Clough? When Mary Elizabeth Grote, before her death, entertained the Vietnamese UNESCO delegate's aunt in Sag Harbor, had she known her husband had just been passed over for promotion to brigadier? And was resentment over that the reason she had subsequently donated twenty-five dollars to a mission hospital in Laos? What were the Bering Straits rendezvous points for missile submarines supporting Ripsaw? Was the transfer of Lieutenant Colonel Carolyn S. Bucknell from Message Center Battalion C.O. to Mess Officer a cover for some CIC complexity? What air support was planned for D plus one? D plus two? Did Major Somebody-or-other's secret drinking account for the curious radio intercept in clear logged at 0834 on 6 October 1985? Or was "Omobray for my eadhay" the code designation for some nefarious scheme to be launched against the gallant, the ever-victorious forces of Neo-Utilitarianism?

Kramer was alternately cast into despondency by the amount of knowledge his captors displayed and puzzled by the psychotic irrelevance of some of the questions they asked him. But most of all he was afraid. As the hours of Phase Two became days, he became more and more afraid—afraid of Phase Three—and so he was ready for Phase Three when the yutes were ready for him.

Phase Three was physical. They beat the living be-hell out of First Lieutenant John Kramer, and then they shouted at him and starved him and kicked him and threw him into bathtubs filled half with salt and water and half with shaved ice. And then they kicked him in the belly and fed him cathartics by the ounce and it went on for a long time; but that was not the bad thing about Phase Three. Kramer found himself crying most of the time, when he was conscious. He did not *want* to tell them everything he knew about Ripsaw—and thus have them be ready when it came, poised and prepared, and know that maybe 50,000 American lives would be down the drain because the surprise was on the wrong side. But he did not know if he could help himself. He was in constant pain. He thought he might die from the pain. Sometimes people did. But he didn't think much about the pain, or the fear of dying, or even about what would happen if—no, *when* he cracked. What he thought about was what came next. For the bad thing about Phase Three was Phase Four.

He remembered. First they would let him sleep. (He had slept very well that other time, because he hadn't known exactly what the Blank Tanks were like. He didn't think he would sleep so well this time.) Then they would wake him up and feed him quickly, and bandage his worst bruises, and bandage his ears, with cotton tampons dipped in vaseline jelly plugged into them, and bandage his eyes, with light-tight adhesive around them, and bandage his mouth, with something like a boxer's toothguard inside so he couldn't even bite his tongue, and bandage his arms and legs, so he couldn't even move them or touch them together. . . .

And then the short superior-private who was kicking him while he thought all this stopped and talked briefly to a noncom. The two of them helped him to a mattress and left him. Kramer didn't want to sleep, but he couldn't help himself; he slipped off, crying weakly out of his puffed and bloody eyes, because he didn't want to sleep, he wanted to die.

Ten hours later he was back in the Blank Tanks.

Sit back and listen. What do you hear?

Perhaps you think you hear nothing. You are wrong. You discount the sound of a distant car's tires, or the crackle of metal as steam expands the pipes. Listen more carefully to these sounds; others lie under them. From the kitchen there is a grunt and hum as the electric refrigerator switches itself on. You change position; your chair creaks, the leather of your shoes slip-slides with a faint sound. Listen more carefully still and hear the tiny roughness in the main bearing of the electric clock in the next room, or the almost inaudible hum of wind in a television antenna. Listen to yourself: Your heartbeat, your pulse in your chin. The rumble of your belly and the faint grating of your teeth. The susurrus of air entering your nostrils. The rub of thumb against finger.

In the Blank Tanks a man hears nothing at all.

The pressure of the tampons in the ear does not allow stirrup to strike anvil; teeth cannot touch teeth, hands cannot clap, he cannot make a noise if he tries to, or hear it if he did.

That is deafness. The Blank Tanks are more than deafness. In them a man is blind, even to the red fog that reaches through closed eyelids. There is nothing to smell. There is nothing to taste. There is nothing to feel except the swaddling-cloths, and through time the nerve ends tire and stop registering this constant touch.

It is something like being unborn and something like never having been at all. There is nothing, absolutely nothing, and although you are not dead you are not alive either. And there you stay.

Kramer was ready for the Blank Tank and did not at once panic. He remembered the tricks he had employed before. He swallowed his own sputum and it made a gratifying popping sound in his inner ear; he hummed until his throat was raw and gasped through flaring nostrils until he became dizzy. But each sound he was able to produce lasted only a moment. He might have dropped them like snowflakes onto wool. They were absorbed and they died.

It was actually worse, he remembered tardily, to produce a sound because you could not help but listen for the echo and no echo came. So he stopped.

In three years he *must* have acquired some additional resources, he thought. Of course. He had! He settled down to construct a crossword puzzle in his head. Let 1 Across be a tropical South American bird, *hoatzin*. Let 1 Down be a medieval diatonic series of tones, *hexacord*. Let 2 Down be the Asiatic wild ass, or *onagin*, which might make the first horizontal word under 1 Across be, let's see, E - N - . . . well, why not the ligature of couplets in verse writing, or *enjambment*. That would make 3 Down— He began to cry, because he could not remember 1 Across.

Something was nagging at his mind, so he stopped crying and waited for it to take form, but it would not. He thought of General Grote, by now surely aware that his aide had been taken; he thought of the consternation that must be shuddering through all the tentacles of Ripsaw. It was not actually going to be so hard, he thought pathetically, because he didn't actually have to *hold out* against the Blank Tanks, he only had to *wait*. After D day, or better, say, D plus 7, it wouldn't much matter what he told them. Then the divisions would be across. Or not across. Breakthrough or failure, it would be decided by then and he could talk.

He began to count off Ripsaw's division officers to himself, as he had so often seen the names on the morning reports. Catton of the XLIst Armored, with Colonels Bogart, Ripner and Bletterman. M'Cleargh of the Highland & Lowland, with Brigadiers Douglass and McCloud. Leventhal of the Vth Israeli, with Koehne, Meier and—he stopped, because it had occurred to him that he might be speaking aloud. He could not tell. All right. Think of something else.

But what?

There was nothing dangerous about sensory deprivation, he lied. It was only a rest. Nobody was hurting him. Looked at in the right way, it was a chance to do some *solid* thinking like you never got time for in real life—strike that. In *outside* life. For instance, what about freshing up on French irregular verbs? Start with avoir. Tu as, vous avez, nous avons. Voi avete, noi abbiamo, du habst . . . Du habst? How did that get in there? Well, how about poetry?

> It is an Ancient Mariner, and he stops the next of kin.
> The guests are met, the feast is set, and sisters under the skin
> Are rag and bone and hank of hair, and beard and glittering eye
> Invite the sight of patient Night, etherized under the sky.
> I should have been a ragged claw; I should have said 'I love you';
> But—here the brown eyes lower fell—I hate to go above you.
> If Ripsaw fail and yutes prevail, what price Clough's Quaker cannon?
> So Grote—

Kramer stopped himself, barely in time. Were there throat mikes? Were the yutes listening in?

He churned miserably in his cotton bonds, because, as near as he could guess, he had probably been in the Blank Tank for less than an hour. D day, he thought to himself, praying that it was only to himself, was still some six weeks away and a week beyond that was seven. Seven weeks, forty-nine days, eleven hundred and, um, seventy-six hours, sixty-six thousand minutes plus. He had only to wait those minutes out, what about the diary?, and then he could talk all he wanted. Talk, confess, broadcast, anything, what difference would it make then?

He paused, trying to remember. That furtive thought had struggled briefly to the surface but he had lost it again. It would not come back.

He tried to fall asleep. It should have been easy enough. His air was metered and the CO_2 content held to a level that would make him torpid; his wastes catheterized away; water and glucose valved into his veins; he was all but *in utero,* and unborn babies slept, didn't they? Did they? He would have to look in the diary, but it would have to wait until he could remember what thought it was that was struggling for recognition. And that was becoming harder with every second.

Sensory deprivation in small doses is one thing; it even has its therapeutic uses, like shock. In large doses it produces a disorientation of psychotic proportions, a melancholia that is all but lethal; Kramer never knew when he went loopy.

iv

He never quite knew when he went sane again, either, except that one day the fog lifted for a moment and he asked a WAC corporal, "When did I get back to Utah." The corporal had dealt with returning yute prisoners before. She said only: "It's Fort Hamilton, sir. Brooklyn."

He was in a private room, which was bad, but he wore a maroon bathrobe, which was good—at least it meant he was in a hospital instead of an Army stockade. (Unless the private room meant he was in the detention ward of the hospital.)

Kramer wondered what he had done. There was no way to tell, at least not by searching his memory. Everything went into a blurry alternation of shouting relays of yutes and the silence of the Blank Tanks. He was nearly sure he had finally told the yutes everything they wanted to know. The question was, when? He would find out at the court-martial, he thought. Or he might have jotted it down, he thought crazily, in the diary.

Jotted it down in the . . . ?

Diary!

That was the thought that had struggled to come through to the surface!

Kramer's screams brought the corporal back in a hurry, and then two doctors who quickly prepared knockout needles. He fought against them all the way.

"Poor old man," said the WAC, watching him twitch and shudder in unconsciousness. (Kramer had just turned forty.) "Second dose of the Blank Tanks for him, wasn't it? I'm not surprised he's having nightmares." She didn't know that his nightmares were not caused by the Blank Tanks themselves, but by his sudden realization that his last stay in the Tanks was totally unnecessary. It didn't matter what he told the yutes, or when! They had had the diary all along, for it had been on him when Mabry thrust him in the rocket; and all Ripsaw's secrets were in it!

The next time the fog lifted for Kramer it was quick, like the turning on of a light, and he had distorted memories of dreams before it. He thought he had just dreamed that General Grote had been with him. He was alone in the same room, sun streaming in a window, voices outside. He felt pretty good, he thought tentatively, and had no time to think more than that because the door opened and a ward boy looked in, very astonished to find Kramer looking back at him.

"Holy heaven," he said. "Wait there!"

He disappeared. Foolish, Kramer thought. Of course he would wait. Where else would he go?

And then, surprisingly, General Grote did indeed walk in.

"Hello, John," he said mildly, and sat down beside the bed, looking at Kramer. "I was just getting in my car when they caught me."

He pulled out his pipe and stuffed it with tobacco, watching Kramer. Kramer could think of nothing to say. "They said you were all right, John. Are you?"

"I—think so." He watched the general light his pipe. "Funny," he said. "I dreamed you were here a minute ago."

"No, it's not so funny; I was. I brought you a present."

Kramer could not imagine anything more wildly improbable in the world than that the man whose combat operation he had betrayed should bring him a box of chocolates, bunch of flowers, light novel or whatever else was appropriate. But the general glanced at the table by Kramer's bed.

There was a flat, green-leather-covered box on it. "Open it up," Grote invited.

Kramer took out a glittering bit of metal depending from a three-barred ribbon. The gold medallion bore a rampant eagle and lettering he could not at first read.

"It's your D.S.M.," Grote said helpfully. "You can pin it on if you like. I tried," he said, "to make it a Medal of Honor. But they wouldn't allow it, logically enough."

"I was expecting something different," Kramer mumbled foolishly.

Grote laughed. "We smashed them, boy," he said gently. "That is, Mick did. He went straight across Po-

lar Nine, down the Ob with one force and the Yenisei
with another. General Clough's got his forward command in Chebarkul now, loving every minute of it.
Why, I was in Karpinsk myself last week—they let me
get that far—of course, it's a rest area. It was a brilliant, bloody, backbreaking show. Completely suc-
cessful."

Kramer interrupted in sheer horror: "Polar *Nine?*
But that was the cover—the Quaker cannon!"

General Grote looked meditatively at his former
aide. "John," he said after a moment, "didn't you ever
wonder why the card-sorters pulled you out for my
staff? A man who was sure to crack in the Blank
Tanks, because he already had?"

The room was very silent for a moment.

"I'm sorry, John. Well, it worked—had to, you
know; a lot of thought went into it. Novotny's been
relieved. Mick's got his biggest victory, no matter what
happens now; he was the man that led *the* invasion."

The room was silent again.

Carefully Grote tapped out his pipe into a metal
wastebasket. "You're a valuable man, John. Matter of
fact, we traded a major general to get you back."

Silence.

Grote sighed and stood up. "If it's any consolation
to you, you held out four full weeks in the Tanks. Good
thing we'd made sure you had the diary with you. Otherwise our Quaker cannon would have been a bust."

He nodded good-bye and was gone. He was a
good officer, was General Grote. He would use a weapon in any way he had to, to win a fight; but if the
weapon was destroyed, and had feelings, he would
come around to bring it a medal afterwards.

Kramer contemplated his Distinguished Service
Medal for a while. Then he lay back and considered
ringing for a Sunday *Times,* but fell asleep instead.

Novotny was now a sour, angry corps commander
away off on the Baltic periphery because of him; a
million and a half NAAARMY troops were dug in

the heart of the enemy's homeland; the greatest operation of the war was an unqualified success. But when the nurse came in that night, the Quaker cannon—the man who had discovered that the greatest service he could perform for his country was to betray it—was moaning in his sleep.

MUTE INGLORIOUS TAM

Cyril left a fragment about medieval England; it had
no story attached to it, only a few pages of description
and character. It lay in my files for fifteen years, until
I happened to be sitting in a panel discussion with two
or three other s-f writers (Ben Bova, Katherine Mac-
Lean and Gordon Dickson, I think they were) and we
fell to talking about what made a science-fiction
writer what he is. What, I asked, might any of us have
been if we had been born in another place and time?
If we could not possibly have been science-fiction
writers, perhaps because there was no science yet,
maybe because we were illiterate? And then it
occurred to me that it would be fun to write a story
about that; and sometime later it struck me that Cyril's
fragment might fit in well with such a notion; and I
dug it out, and it did.

ON A LATE SATURDAY afternoon in summer, just before the ringing of Angelus, Tam of the Wealdway
straightened from the furrows in his plowed strip of
Oldfield and stretched his cracking joints.

He was a small and dark man, of almost pure
Saxon blood. Properly speaking, his name was only
Tam. There was no need for further identification. He
would never go a mile from a neighbor who had known
him from birth. But sometimes he called himself by
a surname—it was one of many small conceits that
complicated his proper and straightforward life—and

31

he would be soundly whipped for it if his Norman masters ever caught him at it.

He had been breaking clods in the field for fifteen hours, interrupted only by the ringing of the canonical hours from the squat, tiny church, and a mouthful of bread and soft cheese at noon. It was not easy for him to stand straight. It was also not particularly wise. A man could lose his strip for poor tilth, and Tam had come close enough, often enough. But there were times when the thoughts that chased themselves around his head made him forget the steady chop of the wooden hoe, and he would stand entranced, staring toward Lymeford Castle, or the river, or toward nothing at all, while he invented fanciful encounters and impossible prosperings. It was another of Tam's conceits, and a most dangerous one, if it were known. The least it might get him was a cuff from a man-at-arms. The most was a particularly unpleasing death.

Since Salisbury, in Sussex, was flat ground, its great houses were not perched dramatically on crags, like the keeps of robber barons along the Rhine or the grim fortresses of the Scottish lairds. They were the least they could be to do the job they had to do, in an age which had not yet imagined the palace or the cathedral.

In the year 1303 Lymeford Castle was a dingy pile of stone. It housed Sir and Lady Robert Bowen (sometimes they spelled it Bohun, or Beauhun, or Beauhaunt) and their household servants and men-at-arms in very great discomfort. It did not seem so to them particularly. They had before them the housing of their Saxon subjects to show what misery could be. The castle was intended to guard a bridge across the Lyme River: a key point on the high road from Portsmouth to London. It did this most effectively. William of Normandy, who had taken England by storm a couple of centuries earlier, did not mean for himself or his descendants to be taken in the same way on

another day. So Lymeford Castle had been awarded
to Sir Robert's great-great-great-grandfather on the
condition that he defend it and thereby defend London
as well against invasion on that particular route from
the sea.

That first Bowen had owned more than stones.
A castle must be fed. The castellan and his lady, their
household servants and their armed men could not be
expected to till the field and milk the cows. The found-
er of Sir Robert's line had solved the problem of feeding
the castle by rounding up a hundred of the defeated
Saxon soldiers, clamping iron rings around their necks
and setting them to work at the great task of clearing
the untidy woods which surrounded the castle. After
cleaning and plowing from sunup to sunset the slaves
were free to gather twigs and mud, with which they
made themselves kennels to sleep in. And in that first
year, to celebrate the harvest and to insure a continu-
ing supply of slaves, the castellan led his men-at-arms
on a raid into Salisbury town itself. They drove back
to Lymeford, with whips, about a hundred Saxon girls
and women. After taking their pick, they gave the rest
to the slaves, and the chaplain read a single perfunc-
tory marriage service over the filthy, ring-necked slaves
and the weeping Salisbury women. Since the male
slaves happened to be from Northumbria, while the
women were Sussex bred, they could not understand
each other's dialects. It did not matter. The huts were
enlarged, and next midsummer there was another crop,
this time of babies.

The passage of two centuries had changed things
remarkably little. A Bowen (or Beauhaunt) still
guarded the Portsmouth-London high road. He still took
pride in his Norman blood. Saxons still tilled the soil
for him and if they no longer had the iron collar, or the
name of slaves, they still would dangle from the gal-
lows in the castle courtyard for any of a very large
number of possible offenses against his authority. At
Runnymede, many years before, King John had signed

the Great Charter conferring some sort of rule of law to protect his barons against arbitrary acts, but no one had thought of extending those rights to the serfs. They could die for almost anything or for nothing at all: for trying to quit their master's soil for greener fields; for failing to deliver to the castle their bushels of grain, as well as their choicest lambs, calves and girl-children; for daring in any way to flout the divine law that made one kind of man ruler and another kind ruled. It was this offense to which Tam was prone, and one day, as his father had told him the day before he died, it would cost him the price that no man can afford to pay, though all do.

Though Tam had never even heard of the Magna Carta, he sometimes thought that a world might sometime come to be in which a man like himself might own the things he owned as a matter of right and not because a man with a sword had not decided to take them from him. Take Alys his wife. He did not mind in any real sense that the men-at-arms had bedded her before he had. She was none the worse for it in any way that Tam could measure; but he had slept badly that night, pondering why it was that no one needed to consult him about the woman the priest had sworn to him that day, and whether it might not be more—more—he grappled for a word ("fair" did not occur to him) and caught at "right"—more right that he should say whose pleasures his property served.

Mostly he thought of sweeter and more fanciful things. When the falconers were by, he sometimes stole a look at the hawk stooping on a pigeon and thought that a man might fly if only he had the wings and the wit to move them. Pressed into driving the castellan's crops into the granary, he swore at the dumb oxen and imagined a cart that could turn its wheels by itself. If the Lyme in flood could carry a tree bigger than a house faster than a man could run, why could that power not pull a plow? Why did a man have to plant five kernels of corn to see one come up? Why could not all five come up and make him five times as fat?

He even looked at the village that was his home, and wondered why it had to be so poor, so filthy and so small; and that thought had hardly occurred even to Sir Robert himself.

In the year 1303 Lymeford looked like this:

The Lyme River, crossed by the new stone structure that was the fourth Lymeford Bridge, ran south to the English Channel. Its west bank was overgrown with the old English oak forest. Its right bank was the edge of the great clearing. Lymeford Castle, hard by the bridge, covered the road and curved northeast to London. For the length of the clearing, the road was not only the king's highway, it was also the Lymeford village street. At a discreet distance from the castle it began to be edged with huts, larger or smaller as their tenants were rich or fecund. The road widened a bit halfway to the edge of the clearing, and there on its right side sat the village church.

The church was made of stone, but that was about all you could say for it. All the wealth it owned it had to draw from the village, and there was not much wealth there to draw. Still, silver pennies had to be sent regularly to the bishop, who in turn would send them on to Rome. The parish priest of Lymeford was an Italian who had never seen the bishop, to whom it had never occurred to try to speak the language and who had been awarded the living of Lymeford by a cardinal who was likewise Italian and likewise could not have described its location within fifty miles. There was nothing unusual in that, and the Italian collected the silver pennies while his largely Norman, but Saxon speaking, locum tenens scraped along on donations of beer, dried fish and the odd occasional calf. He was a dour man who would have been a dreadful one if he had had a field of action that was larger than Lymeford.

Across the street from the church was The Green, a cheerless trampled field where the compulsory archery

practice and pike drill were undergone by every physi-
cally able male of Lymeford, each four weeks, except
in the worst of winter and when plowing or harvest
was larger in Sir Robert's mind than the defense of his
castle. His serfs would fight when he told them to, and
he would squander their lives with the joy a man feels
in exercising the one extravagance he permits himself
on occasion. But that was only at need, and the fields
and the crops were forever. He saw to the crops with
some considerable skill. A three-field system prevailed
in Lymeford. There was Oldfield, east of the road, and
the first land brought under cultivation by the slaves
two hundred years ago. There was Newfield, straddling
the road and marked off from Oldfield by a path into
the woods called the Wealdway, running southeast from
The Green into the oak forest at the edge of the clearing. There was Fallowfield, last to be cleared and
planted, which for the most part lay south of the road
and the castle. From the left side of the road to the
river, The Mead spread its green acres. The Mead
was held in common by all the villagers. Any man
might turn his cows or sheep to graze on it anywhere.
The farmed fields, however, were divided into long,
narrow strips, each held by a villager who would defend it with his fists or his sickle against the encroach-
ment of a single inch. In the year 1303 Oldfield and
Newfield were under cultivation, and Fallowfield was
being rested. Next year it would be Newfield and Fallowfield farmed, and Oldfield would rest.

    While Angelus clanged on the cracked church
bell, Tam stood with his head downcast. He was supposed to be praying. In a way he was, the impenetrable
rote-learned Latin slipping through his brain like the
reiteration of a mantra, but he was also pleasantly occupied in speculating how plump his daughter might
become if they could farm all three fields each year
without destroying the soil, and at the same time thinking of the pot of fennel-spiced beer that should be
waiting in his hut.

As the Angelus ceased to ring, his neighbor's hail dispelled both dreams.

Irritated, Tam shouldered his wooden-bladed hoe and trudged along the Wealdway, worn deep by two hundred years of bare peasant feet.

His neighbor, Hud, fell in with him. In the bastard MidlandSussex hybrid that was the Lymeford dialect, Hud said, "Man, that was a long day."

"All the days are long in the summer."

"You were dreaming again, man. Saw you."

Tam did not reply. He was careful of Hud. Hud was as small and dark as himself, but thin and nervous rather than blocky. Tam knew he got that from his father Robin, who had got it from his mother Joan —who had got it from some man-at-arms on her wedding night spent in the castle. Hud was always asking, always talking, always seeking new things. But when Tam, years younger, had dared to try to open his untamable thoughts to him, Hud had run straight to the priest.

"Won't the players be coming by this time of year, man?" he pestered.

"They might."

"Ah, wouldn't it be a great thing if they came by tomorrow? And then after Mass they'd make their pitch in The Green, and out would come the King of England and Captain Slasher and the Turkish Champion in their clothes colored like the sunset, and St. George in his silver armor!"

Tam grunted. " 'Tisn't silver. Couldn't be. If it was silver the robbers in the Weald would never let them get this far."

The nervous little man said, "I didn't mean it *was* silver. I meant it *looked* like silver."

Tam could feel anger welling up in him, drowning the good aftertaste of his reverie and the foretaste of his fennel beer. He said angrily, "You talk like a fool."

"Like a fool, is it? And who is always dreaming the sun away, man?"

"God's guts, leave off!" shouted Tam, and clamped his teeth on his words too late. He seldom swore. He could have bitten his tongue out after he uttered the words. Now there would be confession of blasphemy to make, and Father Bloughram, who had been looking lean and starved of late, would demand a penance in grain instead of any beggarly saying of prayers. Hud cowered back, staring. Tam snarled something at him, he could not himself have said what, and turned off the deep-trodden path into his own hut.

The hut was cramped and murky with wood smoke from its open hearth. There was a smoke hole in the roof that let some of it out. Tam leaned his hoe against the wattled wall, flopped down onto the bundle of rags in the corner that was the bed for all three of the members of his family and growled at Alys his wife: "Beer." His mind was full of Hud and anger, but slowly the rage cooled and the good thoughts crept back in: Why not a softer bed, a larger hut? Why not a fire that did not smoke, as his returning grandfather, who wore a scar from the Holy Land to his grave, had told him the Saracens had? And with the thought of a different kind of life came the thought of beer; he could taste the stuff now, sluicing the dust from his throat; the bitterness of the roasted barley; the sweetness of the fennel. "Beer," he called again, and became aware that his wife had been tiptoeing about the hut.

"Tam," she said apprehensively, "Joanie Brewer's got the flux."

His brows drew together like thunderclouds. "No beer?" he asked.

"She's got the flux, and not for all the barley in Oldfield could she brew beer. I tried to borrow from Hud's wife, and she had only enough for him, she showed me—"

Tam got up and knocked her spinning into a corner with one backhanded blow. "Was there no beer yesterday?" he shouted. "God forgive you for being the useless slut you are! May the Horned Man and all his brood fly away with a miserable wretch that won't brew beer for the husband that sweats his guts out from sunup to sunset!"

She got up cringing, and he knocked her into the corner again.

The next moment that was a solid crack across his back, and he crashed to the dirt floor. Another blow took him on the legs as he rolled over, and he looked up and saw the raging face of his daughter Kate and the wooden-bladed hoe upraised in her hands.

She did not strike him a third time, but stood there menacingly. "Will you leave her alone?" she demanded.

"Yes, you devil's get!" Tam shouted from the floor, and then, "You'd like me to say no, wouldn't you? And then you'd beat in the brains of the old fool that gave you a name and a home."

Weeping, Alys protested, "Don't say that, husband. She's your child, I'm a good woman, I have nothing black on my soul."

Tam got to his feet and brushed dirt from hs leather breeches and shirt. "We'll say no more about it," he said. "But it's hard when a man can't have his beer."

"You wild boar," said Kate, not lowering the hoe. "If I hadn't come back from The Mead with the cow, you might have killed her."

"No, child," Tam said uneasily. He knew his temper. "Let's talk of other things." Contemptuously she put down the hoe, while Alys got up, sniffling, and began to stir the peaseporridge on the hearth. Suddenly the smoke and heat inside the hut was more than Tam could bear, and muttering something, he stumbled outside and breathed in the cool air of the night.

It was full dark now and, for a wonder, stars were out. Tam's Crusader grandfather had told him of the great bright nights in the mountains beyond Acre, with

such stars that a man could spy friend's face from foe's
at a bowshot. England had nothing like that, but Tam
could make out the Plow, fading toward the sunset, and
Cassiopeia pursuing it from the east. His grandfather
had tried to teach him the Arabic names for some of
the brighter stars, but the man had died when Tam
was ten and the memories were gone. What were
those two, now, so bright and so close together? Something about twin peacocks? Twins at least, thought
Tam, staring at Gemini, but a thought of peacocks
lingered. He wished he had paid closer attention to the
old man, who had been a Saracen's slave for nine
years until a lucky raid had captured his caravan and
set him free.

A distant sound of yelping caught his ear. Tam
read the sound easily enough; a vixen and her half-
grown young, by the shrillness. The birds came into
the plowed fields at night to steal the seed, and the
foxes came to catch the birds, and this night they had
found something big enough to try to catch them—
wolf, perhaps, Tam thought, though it was not like
them to come so near to men's huts in good weather.
There were a plenty of them in Sir Robert's forest,
with fat deer and birds and fish beyond counting in the
streams; but it was what a man's life was worth to take
them. He stood there, musing on the curious chance
that put venison on Sir Robert's table and peaseporridge on his, and on the lights in the sky, until he
realized Alys had progressed from abject to angry and
must by now be eating without him.

After the evening meal Alys scurried over to Hud's
wife with her tale of beastly husbands, and Kate sat
on a billet of wood, picking knots out of her hair.

Tam squatted on the rags and studied her. At fifteen years, or whatever she was, she was a wild one.
How had it happened that the babe who cooed and
grasped at the grass whistle her father made her had
turned into this stranger? She was not biddable. Ed-

wy's strip adjoined Tam's in Fallowfield, and Edwy
had a marriageable son. What was more reasonable
than that Kate should marry him? But she had talked
about his looks. True, the boy was no beauty. What
did that matter? When, as a father should, he had
brushed that aside, she had threatened plainly to run
away, bringing ruin and the rope on all of them. Nor
would she let herself be beaten into good sense, but
instead kicked—with painful accuracy—and bit and
scratched like a fiend from hell's pit.

He felt a pang at that thought. Oh, Alys was an
honest woman. But there were other ways the child
of another could be fobbed off on you. A moment of
carelessness when you didn't watch the cradle—it was
too awful to think of, but sometimes you had to think
of it. Everybody knew that Old People liked nothing
better than to steal somebody's baby and slip one of
their own into the cradle. He and Alys had duly left
bowls of milk out during the child's infancy, and on
feast days bowls of beer. They had always kept a bit
of iron by Kate, because the Old People hated iron.
But still. . . .

Tam lighted a rushlight soaked in mutton fat at
what was left of the fire. Alys would have something
to say about his extravagance, but a mood for talking
was on him, and he wanted to see Kate's face. "Child,"
he said, "one Sunday now the players will come by
and pitch on The Green. And we'll all go after Mass
and see them play. Why, St. George looks as if he
wears armor all of silver!"

She tugged at her hair and would not speak or
look at him.

He squirmed uncomfortably on the ragged bed.
"I'll tell you a story, child," he offered.

Contemptuously, "Tell your drunken friend. I've
heard the two of you, Hud and yourself, lying away
at each other with the beer working in you."

"Not that sort of story, Kate. A story no one has
ever told."

No answer, but at least her face was turned toward him. Emboldened, he began:

" 'Tis a story of a man who owned a great strong wain that could move without oxen, and in it he—"

"What pulled it, then? Goats?"

"Nothing pulled it, child. It moved by itself. It—" he fumbled, and found inspiration—"it was a gift from the Old People, and the man put on it meal and dried fish and casks of water, and he rode in it to one of those bright stars you see just over church. Many days he traveled, child. When he got there—"

"What road goes to a star, man?"

"No road, Kate. This wain rode in the air, like a cloud. And then—"

"Clouds can't carry casks of water," she announced. "You talk like Edwy's mad son that thinks he saw the Devil in a turnip."

"Listen now, Kate!" he snapped. "It is only a story. When the man came to—"

"Story! It's a great silly lie."

"Neither lie nor truth," he roared. "It is a story I am telling you."

"Stories should be sense," she said positively. "Leave off your dreaming, father. All Lymeford talks of it, man. Even in the castle they speak of mad Tam the dreamer."

"Mad, I am?" he shouted, reaching for the hoe. But she was too quick for him. She had it in her hands; he tried to take it from her, and they wrestled, rock against flame, until he heard his wife's caterwauling from the entrance, where she'd come running, called by the noise; and when he looked round, Kate had the hoe from him and space to use it and this time she got him firmly atop the skull—and he knew no more that night.

In the morning he was well enough, and Kate was wisely nowhere in sight. By the time the long day was through he had lost the anger.

Alys made sure there was beer that night, and the nights that followed. The dreams that came from the brew were not the same as the dreams he had tried so hard to put into words. For the rest of his life, sometimes he dreamed those dreams again, immense dreams, dreams that—had he had the words, and the skill, and above all the audience—a hundred generations might have remembered. But he didn't have any of those things. Only the beer.

THE WORLD OF
MYRION FLOWERS

"The World of Myrion Flowers" touched on touchy subjects and, although most of the comments it has drawn since it was first published have been encouraging, there were some that were not. One was that white writers should not write about black characters. In a way, I agree with that; but in the late 1950's there weren't any black writers writing science fiction. One of the nice things about the last decade or so is that that is no longer true.

THE WORLD of Myrion Flowers, which was the world of the American Negro, was something like an idealized England and something like the real Renaissance. As it is in some versions of England, all the members of the upper class were at least friends of friends. Any Harlem businessman knew automatically who was the new top dog in the music department of Howard University a week after an upheaval of the faculty. And as it was in the Florence of Cellini, there was room for versatile men. An American Negro could be a doctor-builder-educator-realist-politician. Myrion Flowers was. Boston-born in 1913 to a lawyer-realist-politician father and a glamorous show-biz mother, he worked hard, drew the lucky number and was permitted to enter the schools which led to an M.D. and a license to practice in the State of New York. Power vacuums occurred around him during the years that followed, and willy-nilly he filled them. A construction firm going to waste, needing a little capital and a little common sense—what could he do? He did it, and accepted its stock. The school board coming to him as a sound man to represent "Ah, your people"? He was a sound man. He served the board well. A trifling examination to pass for a real-estate license—trifling to him who had memorized a dozen textbooks in pathology, histology, anatomy and materia medica—why not? And if they would deem it such a favor if he spoke for the Fusion candidate, why should he not speak, and if they should later invite him to submit names to fill one dozen minor patronage jobs, why should he not give him the names of the needy persons he knew?

Flowers was a cold, controlled man. He never married. In lieu of children he had protégés. These began as Negro kids from orphanages or hopelessly destitute families; he backed them through college and postgraduate schools as long as they worked to the limit of what he considered their abilities; at the first sign of a let-down he axed them. The mortality rate over the years was only about one nongraduate in four —Myrion Flowers was a better predictor of success than any college admissions committee. His successes numbered forty-two when one of them came to him with a brand-new Ph.D. in clinical psychology and made a request.

The protégé's name was Ensal Brubacker. He took his place after dinner in the parlor of Dr. Flowers's Brooklyn brownstone house along with many other suppliants. There was the old woman who wanted an extension of her mortgage and would get it; there was the overstocked appliance dealer who wanted to be bailed out and would not be; there was the mother whose boy had a habit and the husband whose wife was acting stranger and stranger every day; there was the landlord hounded by the building department; there was the cop who wanted a transfer; there was the candidate for the bar who wanted a powerful name as a reference; there was a store-front archbishop who wanted only to find out whether Dr. Flowers was right with God.

Brubacker was admitted to the doctor's study at 9:30. It was only the sixth time he had seen the man who had picked him from an orphanage and laid out some twenty thousand dollars for him since. He found him more withered, colder and quicker than ever.

The doctor did not congratulate him. He said, "You've got your degree, Brubacker. If you've come to me for advice, I'd suggest that you avoid the academic life, especially in the Negro schools. I know what you should do. You may get nowhere, but I would like to see you try one of the Four-A advertising and public relations firms, with a view to becoming a motivational research man. It's time one Negro was working in the higher levels of Madison Avenue, I believe."

Brubacker listened respectfully, and when it was time for him to reply he said: "Dr. Flowers, I'm very grateful of course for everything you've done. I sincerely wish I could— Dr. Flowers, I want to do research. I sent you my dissertation, but that's only the beginning—"

Myrion Flowers turned to the right filing card in his mind and said icily, "The Correlation of Toposcopic Displays, Beta-Wave Amplitudes and Perception of Musical Chord Progressions in 1,107 Unselected Adolescents. Very well. You now have your sandwich board with 'P,' 'H' and 'D' painted on it, fore and aft. I expect that you will now proceed to the job for which you have been trained."

"Yes, sir. I'd like to show you a—"

"I do not," said Dr. Flowers, "want you to be a beloved old George Washington Carver humbly bending over his reports and test tubes. Academic research is of no immediate importance."

"No, sir. I—"

"The power centers of America," said Dr. Flowers, "are government, where our friend Mr. Wilkins is

ably operating, and the executive levels of the large
corporations, where I am attempting to achieve what
is necessary. I want you to be an executive in a large
corporation, Brubacker. You have been trained for
that purpose. It is now perhaps barely possible for you
to obtain a foothold. It is inconceivable to me that you
will not make the effort, neither for me or for your
people."

Brubacker looked at him in misery, and at last
put his face into his hands. His shoulders shook.

Dr. Flowers said scornfully: "I take it you are
declining to make that effort. Good-bye, Brubacker.
I do not want to see you again."

The young man stumbled from the room, carrying a large pigskin valise which he had not been permitted to open.

As he had expected to overwhelm his benefactor
with what he had accomplished he had made no plans
for this situation. He could think only of returning to
the university he had just left where, perhaps, before his little money ran out, he might obtain a grant.
There was not really much hope of that. He had filed no
proposals and sought no advice.

It did not help his mood when the overnight coach
to Chicago was filling up in Grand Central. He was
among the first and took a window seat. Thereafter
the empty place beside him was spotted gladly by lug-
gage-burdened matrons, Ivy-League-clad youngsters,
harrumphing paper-box salesmen—gladly spotted—
and then uncomfortably skimmed past when they discovered that to occupy it they would have to sit next
to the gorilla-rapist-illiterate-tapdancer-mugger-men-
ace who happened to be Dr. Ensal Brubacker.

But he was spared loneliness at the very last. The
fellow who did drop delightedly into the seat beside
him as the train began to move was One of His Own
Kind. That is, he was unwashed, unlettered, a quarter
drunk on liquor that had never known a tax stamp,

and agonizingly high-spirited. He spoke such pure Harlem jive that Brubacker could not understand one word in twenty.

But politeness and a terror of appearing superior forced Brubacker to accept, at 125th Street, a choking swallow from the flat half-pint bottle his seamate carried. And both of these things, plus an unsupportable sense of something lost, caused him to accept his seatmate's later offer of more paralyzing pleasures. In ten months Brubacker was dead, in Lexington, Kentucky, of pneumonia incurred while kicking the heroin habit, leaving behind him a badly puzzled staff doctor. "They'll say everything in withdrawal," he confided to his wife, "but I wonder how this one ever heard the word 'cryptesthesia.' "

It was about a month after that that Myrion Flowers received the package containing Brubacker's effects. There had been no one else to send them to.

He was shaken, that controlled man. He had seen many folk-gods of his people go the same route, but they were fighters, entertainers or revivalists; he had not expected it of a young, brilliant university graduate. For that reason he did not immediately throw the junk away, but mused over it for some minutes. His next visitor found him with a silvery-coppery sort of helmet in his hands.

Flowers's next visitor was a former Corporation Counsel to the City of New York. By attending Dr. Powell's church and having Dr. Flowers take care of his health he kept a well-placed foot in both the principal political camps of the city. He no longer much needed political support, but Flowers had pulled him through one coronary and he was too old to change doctors. "What have you got there, Myrion?" he asked.

Flowers looked up and said precisely, "If I can believe the notes of the man who made it, it is a receiver and amplifier for beta-wave oscillations."

The Corporation Counsel groaned, "God preserve

me from the medical mind. What's that in English?"
But he was surprised to see the expression of wondering awe that came onto Flowers's withered face.

"It reads thoughts," Flowers whispered.

The Corporation Counsel at once clutched his chest, but found no pain. He complained testily, "You're joking."

"I don't think I am, Wilmot. The man who constructed this device had all the appropriate dignities —summa cum laude, Dean's List, interviewed by mail by nearly thirty prospective employers. Before they found out the color of his skin, of course. No," he said reflectively, "I don't think I'm joking, but there's one way to find out."

He lifted the helmet toward his head. The Corporation counsel cried out, "Damn you, Myrion, don't do that!"

Flowers paused. "Are you afraid I'll read your mind and learn your secrets?"

"At my time of life? When you're my doctor? No, Myrion, but you ought to know I have a bad heart. I don't want you electrocuted in front of my eyes. Besides, what the devil does a Negro want with a machine that will tell him what people are thinking? Isn't guessing bad enough for you?"

Myrion Flowers chose to ignore the latter part of what his patient had said. "I don't expect it to electrocute me, and I don't expect this will affect your heart, Wilmot. In any event, I don't propose to be wondering about this thing for any length of time, I don't want to try it when I'm alone and there's no one else here." He plopped the steel bowl on his head. It fit badly and was very heavy. An extension cord hung from it, and without pausing Flowers plugged it into a wall socket by his chair.

The helmet whined faintly and Flowers leaped to his feet. He screamed.

The Corporation Counsel moved rapidly enough to make himself gasp. He snatched the helmet from

Flowers's head, caught him by the shoulders and lowered him into his chair again. "You all right?" he growled.

Flowers shuddered epileptically and then controlled himself. "Thank you, Wilmot. I hope you haven't damaged Dr. Brubacker's device." And then suddenly, "It hit me all at once. It *hurt!*"

He breathed sharply and sat up.

From one of his desk drawers he took a physicians' sample bottle of pills and swallowed one without water. "Everyone was screaming at once," he said. He started to replace the pills, then saw the Corporation Counsel holding his chest and mutely offered him one.

Then he seemed startled.

He looked into his visitor's eyes. "I can still hear you."

"What?"

"It's a false angina, I think. But take the pill. But—" he passed a hand over his eyes—"You thought I was electrocuted, and you wondered how to straighten out my last bill. It's a fair bill, Wilmot. I didn't overcharge you." Flowers opened his eyes very wide and said, "The newsboy on the corner cheated me out of my change. He—" He swallowed and said, "The cops in the squad car just turning off Fulton Street don't like my having white patients. One of them is thinking about running in a girl that came here." He sobbed, "It didn't stop, Wilmot."

"For Christ's sake, Myrion, lie down."

"It didn't stop. It's not like a radio. You can't turn it off. Now I can hear—everybody! Every mind for miles around *is pouring into my head* WHAT IT THINKS ABOUT ME—ABOUT ME—ABOUT US!"

Ensal Brubacker, who had been a clinical psychologist and not a radio engineer, had not intended his helmet to endure the strain of continuous operation nor had he thought to provide circuit-breakers. It had been meant to operate for a few moments at most, enough to reroute a few neurons, open a blocked path or two. One of its parts overheated. Another took too much load as a result, and in a moment the thing was afire. It blew the fuses and the room was in darkness. The elderly ex-Corporation Counsel managed to get the fire out, and then picked up the phone. Shouting to be heard over the screaming of Myrion Flowers, he summoned a Kings County ambulance. They knew Flowers's name. The ambulance was there in nine minutes.

Flowers died some weeks later in the hospital—not Kings County, but he did not know the difference. He had been under massive sedation for almost a month until it became a physiological necessity to taper him off; and as soon as he was alert enough to do so he contrived to hang himself in his room.

His funeral was a state occasion. The crowds were enormous and there was much weeping. The Corporation Counsel was one of those permitted to cast a clod of earth upon the bronze casket, but he did not weep.

No one had ever figured out what the destroyed instrument was supposed to have been, and Wilmot did not tell. There are inventions and inventions, he thought, and reading minds is a job for white men. If even for white men. In the world of Myrion Flowers many seeds might sturdily grow, but some ripe fruits would mature into poison.

No doubt the machine might have broken any mind, listening in on every thought that concerned one. It was maddening and dizzying, and the man who wore the helmet would be harmed in any world; but only in the world of Myrion Flowers would he be hated to death.

THE GIFT OF GARIGOLLI

This is the last story of the posthumous collaborations to be published, and in one sense it is the most dated of them. It is a pretty *damn* sexist story. Shirl is Dorothy Vaneman Seaton out of Anita Loos: pretty, kind, charming and possessed of the I.Q. of a toad. Nobody would have written this story in the 1970's, not Cyril, and certainly not I, and over a good many years I would from time to time look at the tattered manuscript again and try to find some way of detoxifying it. There never was one. There was a great deal of brightness and charm, but it was all bound up in the empty-headedness of Shirl. I couldn't change that without destroying everything Cyril had put on paper, and so I finally took my courage in my hands, pretended that it was 1953 instead of 1973 and finished it up.

Garigolli to Home Base
Greeting, Chief,
I'm glad you're pleased with the demographics and cognitics studies. You don't mention the orbital mapping, but I suppose that's all complete and satisfactory.

Now will you please tell me how we're going to get off this lousy planet?

Keep firmly in mind, Chief, that we're not complainers. You don't have a better crew anywhere in the Galaxy and you know it. We've complied with the Triple Directive, every time, on every planet we've explored. Remember Arcturus XII? But this time we're having trouble. After all, look at the disproportion in mass. And take a look at the reports we've sent in. These are pretty miserable sentients, Chief.

So will you let us know, please, if there has ever been an authorized exception to Directive Two? I don't mean we aren't going to bust a link to comply— if we can—but frankly, at this moment, I don't see how.

And we need to get out of here fast.

Garigolli

Although it was a pretty morning in June, with the blossoms dropping off the catalpa trees and the algae blooming in the twelve-foot plastic pool, I was not enjoying either my breakfast or the morning mail.

The letter from the lawyer started, the way letters from lawyers do, with

RE: GUDSELL VS. DUPOIR

and went on to advise Dupoir (that's me, plus my wife and our two-year-old son Butchie) that unless a certified check arrived in Undersigned's office before close of business June 11th (that was tomorrow) in the amount of $14,752.03, Undersigned would be compelled to institute Proceedings at once.

I showed it to my wife, Shirl, for lack of anything better to do.

She read it and nodded intelligently. "He's really been very patient with us, considering," she said. "I suppose this is just some more lawyer-talk?"

It had occurred to me, for a wild moment, that maybe she had $14,752.03 in the old sugar bowl as a surprise for me, but I could see she didn't. I shook my head. "This means they take the house," I said. "I'm not mad any more. But you won't sign anything for your brother after this, will you?"

"Certainly not," she said, shocked. "Shall I put that letter in the paper-recycling bin?"

"Not just yet," I said, taking off my glasses and hearing aid. Shirl knows perfectly well that I can't hear her when my glasses are off, but she kept on talking anyway as she wiped the apricot puree off Butchie's chin, rescued the milk glass, rinsed the plastic infant-food jar and dropped it in the "plastics" carton, rinsed the lid and put it in the "metals" box and poured my coffee. We are a very ecological household. It astonishes me how good Shirl is at things like that, considering.

I waved fruit flies away from the general direction of my orange juice and put my glasses back on in time to catch her asking, wonderingly, "What would they do with our house? I mean, I'm not a demon decorator like Ginevra Freedman. I just like it comfortable and neat."

"They don't exactly want the house," I explained. "They just want the money they'll get after they sell it to somebody else." Her expression cleared at once. Shirl always likes to understand things.

I sipped my coffee, fending off Butchie's attempt to grab the cup, and folded the letter and laid it across my knees like an unsheathed scimitar, ready to taste the blood of the *giaour,* which it kind of was. Butchie indicated that he would like to eat it, but I didn't see that that would solve the problem. Although I didn't have any better way of solving it, at that.

I finished the orange juice, patted Butchie's head and, against my better judgment, gave Shirl the routine kiss on the nose.

"Well," she said, "I'm glad that's settled. Isn't it nice the way the mail comes first thing in the morning now?"

I said it was very nice and left for the bus but, really, I could have been just as happy if Undersigned's letter had come any old time. The fruit flies were pursuing me all the way down the street. They seemed to think they could get nourishment out of me, which suggested that fruit flies were about equal in intelligence to brothers-in-law. It, was not a surprising thought. I had thought it before.

> Garigolli to Home Base
> Chief,
> The mobility of this Host is a constant pain in the spermatophore. Now he's gone off on the day-cycle early, and half the crew are still stuck in his domicile. Ultimate Matrix knows how they'll handle it if we don't get back before they run out of group empathy.
> You've got no reason to take that tone, Chief. We're doing a good job and you know it. "Directive One: To remain undetected by sentients on planet being explored." A hundred and forty-four p.g., right? They don't have a clue we're here, although I concede that that part is fairly easy, since they are so much bigger than we are. "Directive Three: Subject to Directives One and Two, to make a complete study of geographic, demographic, ecological and cognitic factors and to transmit same to Home Base." You actually complimented us on those! It's only Directive Two that's giving us trouble.
> We're still trying, but did it ever occur to you that maybe these people don't *deserve* Directive Two?
> *Garigolli*

I loped along the jungle trail to the bus stop, calculating with my razor-sharp mind that the distance from the house was almost exactly 14,752.03 centimeters. As centimeters it didn't sound bad at all. As money, $14,752.03 was the kind of sum I hadn't written down since Commercial Arithmetic in P.S. 98.

I fell in with Barney Freedman, insurance underwriter and husband of Ginevra, the Demon Decorator. "Whatever became of Commercial Arithmetic?" I asked him. "Like ninety-day notes for fourteen thousand seven hundred and fifty-two dollars and three cents at six percent simple interest? Although why anybody would be dumb enough to lend anybody money for ninety days beats me. If he doesn't have it now, he won't have it in ninety days."

"You're in some kind of trouble."

"Shrewd guess."

"So what did Shirl do now?"

"She co-signed a note for her brother," I said. "When he went into the drying-out sanitarium for the gold treatment. They wouldn't take him on his own credit, for some reason. They must have gold-plated him. He said the note was just a formality, so Shirl didn't bother me with it."

We turned the corner. Barney said, "Ginerva didn't bother me once when the telephone company——"

"So when Shirl's brother got undrunk," I said, "he told her not to worry about it and went to California. He thought he might catch on with the movies."

"Did he?"

"He didn't even catch cold with the movies. Then they sent us the bill. Fourteen thou—well, they had it all itemized. Three nurses. Medication. Suite. Occupational Therapy. Professional services. Hydrotherapy. Group counseling. One-to-one counseling. Limousine. Chauffeur for limousine. Chauffeur's helper for limousine. Chauffeur's helper's hard-boiled eggs for lunch. Salt for chauffeur's helper's hard-boiled——"

"You're getting hysterical," Barney said. "You mean he just skipped?" We were at the bus stop, with a gaggle of other prosperous young suburbanites.

I said, "Like a flat rock on a pond. So we wrote him, and of course the letters came back. They didn't fool around, the Institute for Psychosomatic Adjustment didn't."

"That's a pretty name."

"I telephoned a man up there to explain, when we got the first letter. He didn't sound pretty. Just tired. He said my wife shouldn't sign things without reading them. And he said if his house was—something about joint tenancy in fee simple, he would break his wife's arm if she was the type that signed things without reading them, and keep on rebreaking it until she stopped. Meanwhile they had laid out a lot of goods and services in good faith, and what was I going to do about it?"

The bus appeared on the horizon, emitting jet trails of Diesel smog. We knotted up by the sign. "So I told him I didn't know," I said, "but I know now. I'll get sued, that's what I'll do. The Dupoirs always have an answer to every problem."

Conversation was suspended for fifteen seconds of scrimmage while we entered the bus. Barney and I were lucky. We wound up with our heads jammed affectionately together, not too far from a window that sucked in Diesel fumes and fanned them at us. I could see the fruit flies gamely trying to get back to my ear, but they were losing the battle.

Barney said, "Hey. Couldn't you sell your house to somebody you trusted for a dollar, and then they couldn't—"

"Yes, they could. And then we'd both go to jail. I asked a guy in our legal department."

"Huh." The bus roared on, past knots of other prosperous young suburbanites who waved their fists at us as we passed. "How about this. I hope you won't take this the wrong way. But couldn't there be some angle about Shirl being, uh, not exactly *competent* to sign any kind of—"

"I asked about that too, Barney. No hope. Shirl's never been hospitalized, she's never been to a shrink, she runs a house and a husband and a small boy just fine. Maybe she's a little impulsive. But a lot of people are impulsive, the man said."

Garigolli to Home Base
Chief,
I think we've got it. These people use a medium of exchange, remember? And the Host doesn't have enough of it! What could be simpler?

With a little modification there are a couple of local organisms that should be able to concentrate the stuff out of the ambient environment, and then— And then we're off the impaling spike!

Garigolli

The bus jerked to a stop at the railroad station and we boiled out on successive rollers of humanity which beached us at separate parts of the platform.

The 8:07 slid in at 8:19 sharp and I swung aboard, my mighty thews rippling like those of the giant anthropoids among whom I had been raised. With stealthy tread and every jungle-trained sense alert I stalked a vacant seat halfway down the aisle on the left, my fangs and molars bared, my liana-bound, flint-tipped *Times* poised for the thrust of death. It wasn't my morning. Ug-Fwa the Hyena, scavenger of the mighty Limpopo, bounded from the far vestibule giving voice to his mad cackle and slipped into the vacant seat. I and the rest of the giant anthropoids glared, unfolded our newspapers and pretended to read.

The headlines were very interesting that morning. PRES ASKS $14,752.03 FOR MISSILE DEFENSE. "SLICK" DUPOIR SOUGHT IN DEFAULT CASE. RUMOR RED PURGE OF BROTHER-IN-LAW. QUAKE DEATH TOLL SET AT 14,752.03. BODY OF SKID ROW CHARÁCTER IDENTI-FIED AS FORMER PROSPEROUS YOUNG SUBURBANITE; BROTHER-IN-LAWS FLIES FROM COAST, WEEPS "WHY DIDN'T HE ASK ME FOR HELP?" FOSTER PARENTS OF "BUTCHIE" DUPOIR OPEN LEGAL FIGHT AGAINST DES-TITUTE MA AND PA, SAY "IF THEY LOVE HIM WHY DON'T THEY SUPPORT HIM?" GLIDER SOARS 14,752.-03 MILES. DUPOIR OFF 147.52—no, that was a fly speck, not a decimal point—OFF 14,752.03 FOR NEW LOW, RAILS AND BROTHERS AND LAW MIXED IN ACTIVE TRADING. I always feel you're more efficient if you start the day with the gist of the news straight in your mind.

I arrived at the office punctually at 9:07, late enough to show that I was an executive, but not so late that Mr. Horgan would notice it. The frowning brow of my cave opened under the grim rock front that bore the legend "International Plastics Co." and I walked in, nodding good morning to several persons from the Fourteenth Floor, but being nodded to myself only by Hermie, who ran the cigar stand. Hermie cultivated my company because I was good for a dollar on the numbers two or three times a week. Little did he know that it would be many a long day before he saw a dollar of mine, perhaps as many as 14,752.03 of them.

> Garigolli to Home Base
> Further to my last communication, Chief,
> We ran into a kind of a setback. We found a suitable organic substrate and implanted a colony of modified organisms which extracted gold from environmental sources, and they were performing beautifully, depositing a film of pure metal on the substrate, which the Host was carrying with him.
> Then he folded it up and threw it in a waste receptacle.
> We're still working on it, but I don't know, Chief, I don't know.
>
> *Garigolli*

I find it a little difficult to explain to people what I do for a living. It has something to do with making the country plastics-conscious. I make the country plastics-conscious by writing newspaper stories about plastics which only seem to get printed in neighborhood shopping guides in Sioux Falls, Idaho. And by scripting talk features about plastics which get run from 11:55 P.M. to 12:00 midnight on radio stations the rest of whose programs time is devoted to public-service items like late jockey changes at Wheeling Downs. And by scripting television features which do not seem ever to be run on any station. And by handling the annual Miss Plastics contest, at least up to the point where actual contestants appear, when it is taken over by the people from the Fourteenth Floor. And by writing the monthly page of Plastics Briefs which goes out, already matted, to 2,000 papers in North America. Plastics Briefs is our best bet because each Brief is illustrated by a line drawing of a girl doing something with, to or about plastics, and her costume is always brief. As I said, all this is not easy to explain, so when people ask me what I do I usually say, "Whatever Mr. Horgan tells me to."

This morning Mr. Horgan called me away from a conference with Jack Denny, our Briefs artist, and said: "Dupoir, that Century of Plastics Anniversary Dinner idea of yours is out. The Fourteenth Floor says it lacks thematic juice. Think of something else for a winter promotion, and think big!" He banged a plastic block on his desk with a little plastic hammer.

I said, "Mr. Horgan, how about this? Are we getting the break in the high-school chemistry text books we should? Are we getting the message of polythene to every boy, girl, brother-in-law—"

He shook his head. "That's small," he said, and went on to explain: "By which I mean it isn't big. Also there is the flak we are getting from the nature nuts, which the Fourteenth Floor does not think you are dealing with in a creative way."

"I've ordered five thousand pop-up recycling bins for the test, Mr. Horgan. They're not only plastic, they're *recycle*d plastic. We use them in my own home, and I am confident—"

"Confidence," he said, "is when you've got your eyes so firmly fixed on the goal that you trip on a dog-doodie and fall in the crap."

I regrouped. "I think we can convert the present opposition from the ecology movement to—"

"The ecology movement," he said, "is people who love buzzards better than babies and catfish better than cars."

I fell back on my last line of defense. "Yes, Mr. Horgan," I said.

"Personally," Mr. Horgan said, "I *like* seeing plastic bottles bobbing in the surf. It makes me feel, I don't know, like part of something that is going to last forever. I want you to communicate that feeling, Dupoir. Now go get your Briefs out."

I thought of asking for a salary advance of $14,-752.03, but hesitated.

"Is there something else?"

"No, Mr. Horgan. Thank you." I left quietly.

Jack Denny was still waiting in my office, doodling still-life studies of cornucopias with fruits and nuts spilling out of them. "Look," he said, "how about this for a change? Something symbolic of the season, like 'the rich harvest of Plastics to make life more gracious,' like?"

I said kindly, "You don't understand copy, Jack. Do you remember what we did for last September?"

He scowled. "A girl in halter and shorts, very brief and tight, putting up plastic storm windows."

"That's right. Well, I've got an idea for something kind of novel this year. A little two-act drama. Act One: She's wearing halter and shorts and she's taking down the plastic screens. Act Two: She's wearing a dress and putting up the plastic storm windows. And this is important. In Act Two there's wind, and autumn leaves blowing, and the dress is kind of wind-blown tight against her. Do you know what I mean, Jack?"

He said evenly, "I was the youngest child and only boy in a family of eight. If I didn't know what you meant by now I would deserve to be put away. Sometimes I think I *will* be put away. Do you know what seven older sisters can do to the psychology of a sensitive young boy?" He began to shake.

"Draw, Jack," I told him hastily. To give him a chance to recover himself I picked up his cornucopias. "Very nice," I said, turning them over. "Beautiful modeling. I guess you spilled some paint on this one?"

He snatched it out of my hand. "Where? That? That's gilt. I don't even have any gilt."

"No offense, Jack. I just thought it looked kind of nice." It didn't, particularly, it was just a shiny yellow smear in a corner of the drawing.

"Nice! Sure, if you'd let me use metallic inks. If you'd go to high-gloss paper. If you'd *spend* a few bucks—"

"Maybe, Jack," I said, "it'd be better, at that, if you took these back to your office. You can concentrate better there, maybe."

He went out, shaking.

I stayed in and thought about my house and brother-in-law and the Gudsell Medical Credit Bureau and after a while I began to shake too. Shaking, I phoned a Mr. Klaw, whom I had come to think of as my "account executive" at Gudsell.

Mr. Klaw was glad to hear from me. "You got our lawyer's note? Good, good. And exactly what arrangements are you suggesting, Mr. Dupoir?"

"I don't know," I said openly. "It catches me at a bad time. If we could have an extension—"

"Extensions we haven't got," he said regretfully. "We had one month of extensions, and we gave you the month, and now we're fresh out. I'm really sorry, Dupoir."

"With some time I could get a second mortgage, Mr. Klaw."

"You could at that, but not for $14,752.03."

"Do you want to put me and my family on the street?"

"Goodness, no, Mr. Dupoir! What we want is the sanitarium's money, including our commission. And maybe we want a *little* bit to make people think before they sign things, and maybe that people who should go to the county hospital *go* to the county hospital instead of a frankly de luxe rest home."

"I'll call you later," I said.

"Please do," said Mr. Klaw sincerely.

Tendons slack as the limp lianas, I leafed listlessly through the *dhowani-bark* jujus on my desk, studying Jack Denny's draftsmanship with cornucopias. The yellow stain, I noted, seemed to be spreading, even as a brother-in-law's blood might spread on the sands of the doom-pit when the cobras hissed the hour of judgment.

Mr. Horgan rapped perfunctorily on the doorframe and came in. "I had the impression, Dupoir, that you had something further to ask me at our conference this morning. I've learned to back those judgments, Dupoir."

"Well, sir—" I began.

"Had that feeling about poor old Globus," he went on. "You remember Miss Globus? Crying in the file room one day. Seems she'd signed up for some kind of charm school. Couldn't pay, didn't like it, tried to back out. They wanted their money. Attached her wages. Well. Naturally, we couldn't have that sort of financial irresponsibility. I understand she's a PFC in the WAC now. What was it you wanted, Dupoir?"

"Me, Mr. Horgan? Wanted? No. Nothing at all."

"Glad we cleared that up," he grunted. "Can't do your best work for the firm if your mind's taken up with personal problems. Remember, Dupoir. We want the country plastics conscious, and forget about those ecology freaks."

"Yes, Mr. Horgan."

"And big. Not small."

"Big it is, Mr. Horgan," I said. I rolled up Jack Denny's sketches into a thick wad and threw them at him in the door, but not before he had closed it behind him.

Garigolli to Home Base
Listen Chief,

I appreciate your trying to work out a solution for us, but you're not doing as well as we're doing, even. Not that that's much.

We tried again to meet that constant aura of medium-of-exchange need for the Host, but he destroyed the whole lash-up again. Maybe we're misunderstanding him?

Artifacts are out. He's too big to see anything we make. Energy sources don't look promising. Oh, sure, we could elaborate lesser breeds that would selectively concentrate, for instance, plutonium or one of the uraniums. I don't think this particular Host would know the difference unless the scale was very large, and then, blooie, critical mass.

Meanwhile morale is becoming troublesome. We're holding together, but I wouldn't describe the condition as *good*. Vellitot has been wooing Dinnoliss in spite of the secondary directives against breeding while on exploration missions. I've cautioned them both, but they don't seem to stop. The funny thing is they're both in the male phase.

Garigolli

Between Jack Denny and myself we got about half of the month's Plastics Briefs before quitting time. Maybe they weren't big, but they were real windblown. All factors considered, I don't think it is very much to my discredit that two hours later I was moodily drinking my seventh beer in a dark place near the railroad station.

The bartender respected my mood, the TV was off, the juke box had nothing but blues on it and there was only one fly in my lugubrious ointment, a little man who kept trying to be friendly.

From time to time I gave him a scowl I had copied from Mr. Horgan. Then he would edge down the bar for a few minutes before edging back. Eventually he got up courage enough to talk, and I got too gloomy to crush him with my mighty thews, corded like the jungle-vines that looped from the towering *nganga*-palms.

He was some kind of hotelkeeper, it appeared. "My young friend, you may think you have problems, but there's no business like my business. Mortgage, in-

surance, state supervision, building and grounds maintenance, kitchen personnel and purchasing, linen, uni-
forms, the station wagon and the driver, carpet repairs
—oh, God, carpet repairs! No matter how many ash
trays you put around, you know what they do? They
steal the ashtrays. Then they stamp out cigarettes on
the carpets." He began to weep.

I told the bartender to give him another. How
could I lose? If he passed out I'd be rid of him. If he
recovered I would have his undying, doglike affection
for several minutes, and what kind of shape was I
in to sneer at that?

Besides, I had worked out some pretty interesting
figures. "Did you know," I told him, "that if you spend
$1.46 a day on cigarettes, you can save $14,752.03
by giving up smoking for 10,104 and a quarter days?"

He wasn't listening, but he wasn't weeping any
more either. He was just looking lovingly at his vodka
libre, or whatever it was. I tried a different tack. "When
you see discarded plastic bottles bobbing in the surf,"
I asked, "does it make you feel like part of something grand and timeless that will go on forever?"

He glanced at me with distaste, then went back
to adoring his drink. "Or do you like buzzards better
than babies?" I asked.

"They're all babies," he said. "Nasty, smelly, up-
chucking babies."

"Who are?" I asked, having lost the thread. He
shook his head mysteriously, patted his drink and
tossed it down.

"Root of most evil," he said, swallowing. Then,
affectionately, "Don't know where I'd be with it, don't
know where I'd be without it."

He appeared to be talking about booze. "On your
way home, without it?" I suggested.

He said obscurely, "Digging ditches, without it."
Then he giggled. "Greatest business in the world!
But oh! the worries! The competition! And when you
come down to it it's all just aversion, right?"

"I can see you have a great aversion to liquor," I said politely.

"No, stupid! The *guests*."

Stiffly I signaled for Number Eight, but the bartender misunderstood and brought another for my friend, too. I said, "You have an aversion to the guests?"

He took firm hold on the bar and attempted to look squarely into my eyes, but wound up with his left eye four inches in front of my left eye and both our right eyes staring at respective ears. "The *guests* must be made to feel an aversion to *alcohol*," he said. "Secret of the whole thing. Works. Sometimes. But oh! it costs."

Like the striking fangs of Nag, the cobra, faster than the eye can follow, my trained reflexes swept the beer up to my lips. I drank furiously, scowling at him. "You mean to say you ran a drunk farm?" I shouted.

He was shocked. "My boy! No need to be fulgar. An 'institute,' eh? Let's leave the aversion to the drunks."

"I have to tell you, sir," I declared, "that I have a personal reason for despising all proprietors of such institutions!"

He began to weep again. "You, too! Oh, the general scorn."

"In my case, there is nothing general—"

"—the hatred! The unthinking contempt. And for what?"

I snarled. "For your blood-sucking ways."

"Blood, old boy?" he said, surprised. "No, nothing like that. We don't use blood. We use gold, yes, but the gold cure's old hat. Need new gimmick. Can't use silver, too cheap. Really doesn't matter what you say you use. All aversion—drying them out, keeping them comfy and aversion. But no blood."

He wiggled his fingers for Number Nine. Moodily I drank, glaring at him over my glass.

"In the wrong end of it, I sometimes think," he went on meditatively, staring with suspicious envy at the bartender. *"He* doesn't have to worry. Pour it out, pick up the money. No concern about expensive rooms standing idle, staff loafing around picking their noses, overhead going on, going on—you wouldn't be*lieve* how it goes on, whether the guests are there to pay for it or not—"

"Hah," I muttered.

"You've simply no idea what I go through," he sobbed. "And then they won't pay. No, really. Fellow beat me out of $14,752.03 just lately. I'm taking it out of the co-signer's hide, of course, but after you pay the collection agency, what's the profit?"

I choked on the beer, but he was too deep in sorrow to notice.

Strangling, I gasped, "Did you say fourteen thousand—?"

He nodded. "Seven hundred and fifty-two dollars, yes. And three cents. Astonishes you, doesn't it, the deadbeats in this world?"

I couldn't speak.

"You wouldn't think it," he mourned. "All those salaries. All those rooms. The hydrotherapy tubs. The *water* bill."

I shook my head.

"Probably you think my life's a bowl of roses, hey?"

I managed to pry my larynx open enough to wheeze, "Up to this minute, yes, I did. You've opened my eyes."

"Drink to that," he said promptly. "Hey, barman!"

But before the bartender got there with Number Ten the little man hiccoughed and slid melting to the floor, like a glacier calving into icebergs.

The bartender peered over at him. "Every *damn* night," he grumbled. "And who's going to get him home this time?"

My mind working as fast as *Ngo,* the dancing

spider, spinning her web, I succeeded in saying, "Me. Glad to oblige. Never fear."

> Garigolli to Home Base
> Chief,
> All right, I admit we haven't been exactly 144 p.g. on this project, but there's no reason for you to get loose. Reciting the penalties for violating the Triple Directive is uncalled-for.
> Let me point out that there has been no question at any time of compliance with One or Three. And even Directive Two, well, we've done what we could. "To repay sentients in medium suitable to them for information gained." These sentients are tricky, Chief. They don't seem to empathize, really. See our reports. They often take without giving in return among themselves, and it seems to me that under the circumstances a certain modification of Directive Two would have been quite proper.
> But I am not protesting the ruling. Especially since you've pointed out it won't do any good. When I get old and skinny enough to retire to a sling in Home Base I guess I'll get that home-base mentality too, but way out here on the surface of the exploration volume it looks diflerent, believe me.
> And what is happening with the rest of our crew back at Host's domicile I can't even guess. They must be nearly frantic by now.
> > *Garigolli*

There was some discussion with a policeman he wanted to hit (apparently under the impression that the cop was his night watchman playing hookey), but I finally got the little man to the Institute for Psychosomatic Adjustment.

The mausoleum that had graduated my brother-in-law turned out to be three stories high, with a sun porch and a slate roof and bars on the ground-floor bay windows. It was not all that far from my house. Shirl had been pleased about that, I remembered. She said we could visit her brother a lot there, and in fact she had gone over once or twice on Sundays, but me, I'd never set eyes on the place before.

Dagger-sharp fangs flecking white spume, none dared dispute me as I strode through the great green corridors of the rain forest. Corded thews rippling like pythons under my skin, it was child's play to carry the craven jackal to his lair. The cabbie helped me up the steps with him.

The little man, now revealed as that creature who in anticipation had seemed so much larger and hairier, revived slightly as we entered the reception hall. "Ooooh," he groaned. "Watch the bouncing, old boy. That door. My office. Leather couch. Much obliged."

I dumped him on the couch, lit a green-shaded lamp on his desk, closed the door and considered.

Mine enemy had delivered himself into my power. All I had to do was seize him by the forelock. I seemed to see the faces of my family—Shirl's smiling sweetly, Butchie's cocoa-overlaid-with-oatmeal—spurring me on.

There had to be a way.

I pondered. Life had not equipped me for this occasion. Raffles or Professor Moriarity would have known what to do at once, but, ponder as I would, I couldn't think of anything to do except to go through the drawers of his desk.

Well, it was a start. But it yielded very little. Miscellaneous paper clips and sheaves of letterheads, a carton of cigarettes of a brand apparently flavored with rice wine and extract of vanilla, part of a fifth of Old Rathole and five switchblade knives, presumably taken from the inmates. There was also $6.15 in unused postage stamps, but I quickly computed that, even if I went to the trouble of cashing them in, that would leave me $14,745.88 short.

Of Papers to Burn there were none.

All in all, the venture was a bust. I wiped out a water glass with one of the letterheads (difficult, be-

cause they were of so high quality that they seemed
likelier to shatter than to wad up), and forced down a
couple of ounces of the whiskey (difficult, because it
was of so low).

Obviously anything of value, like for instance co-
signed agreements with brothers-in-law, would be in a
safe, which itself would probably be in the offices of the
Gudsell Medical Credit Bureau. Blackmail? But there
seemed very little to work with, barring one or two
curious photographs tucked in among the envelopes.
Conceivably I could cause him some slight embar-
rassment, but nowhere near $14,752.03 worth. I had
not noticed any evidence of Red espionage that might
put the little man (whose name, I learned from his
letterhead, was Bermingham) away for 10,104 and a
quarter days, while I saved up the price of reclaiming
our liberty.

There seemed to be only one possible thing to do.

Eyes glowing like red coals behind slitted lids, I
walked lightly on velvet-soft pads to the *kraal* of the
witch-man. He was snoring with his mouth open. Totally vulnerable to his doom.

Only, how to inflict it?

It is not as easy as one might think to murder a
person. Especially if one doesn't come prepared for it.
Mr. Horgan doesn't like us to carry guns at the office,
and heaven knows what Shirl would do with one
if I left it around home. Anyway, I didn't have one.

Poison was a possibility. The Old Rathole suggested itself. But we'd already tried that, hadn't we?

I considered the switchblade knives. There was a
technical problem. Would *you* know where the heart
is? Granted, it had to be inside his chest somewhere,
and sooner or later I could find it. But what would I
say to Mr. Bermingham after the first three or four
exploratory stabs woke him up?

The only reasonably efficient method I could think
of to insure Mr. Bermingham's decease was to burn
the place down with him in it. Which, I quickly per-

ceived, meant with whatever cargo of drying-out drunks the Institute now possessed in it too, behind those barred windows.

At this point I came face to face with myself.

I wasn't going to kill anybody. I wasn't going to steal any papers.

What I was going to do was, I was going to let Mr. Klaw's lawyers go ahead and take our house, because I just didn't know how to do anything else. I hefted the switchblades in my hand, threw them against the wall and poured myself another slug of Mr. Bermingham's lousy whiskey, wishing it would kill me right there and be a lesson to him.

Garigolli to Home Base
Now, don't get excited, Chief,
But we have another problem.

Before I get into it, I would like to remind you of a couple of things. First, I was against exploring this planet in the first place, remember? I said it was going to be very difficult, on the grounds of the difference in mass between its dominant species and us. I mean, really. Here we are fighting member to member against dangerous beasts all the time, and the beasts, to the Host and his race, are only microorganisms that live unnoticed in their circulatory systems, their tissues, their food and their environment. Anybody could tell that this was going to be a tough assignment, if not an impossible one.

Then there's the fact that this Host moves around so. I told you some of our crew got left in his domicile. Well, we've timed this before, and almost always he returns within 144 or 216 time-units—at most, half of one of his planet's days. It's pretty close to critical, but our crew is tough and they can survive empathy-deprival that long. Only this time he has been away, so far, nearly 432 time-units. It's bad enough for those of us who have been with him. The ones who were cut off back at his domicile must have been through the tortures of the damned.

Two of them homed in on us to report just a few

time-units ago, and I'm afraid you're not going to like what's happened. They must have been pretty panicky. They decided to try meeting the Second Directive themselves. They modified some microorganisms to provide some organic chemicals they thought the Host might like.

Unfortunately the organisms turned out to have an appetite for some of the Host's household artifacts, and they're pretty well demolished. So we not only haven't *given* him anything to comply with Directive Two, we've *taken* something from him. And in the process maybe we've called attention to ourselves.

I'm giving it to you arced, Chief, because I know that's how you'd like it. I accept full responsibility.

Because I don't have any choice, do I?

Garigolli

"What the Hell," said the voice of Mr. Bermingham, from somewhere up there, "are you doing in my office?"

I opened my eyes, and he was quite right. I was in Mr. Bermingham's office. The sun was streaming through Mr. Bermingham's Venetian blinds, and Mr. Bermingham was standing over me with a selection of the switchblade knives in his hands.

I don't know how Everyman reacts to this sort of situation. I guess I ran about average. I pushed myself up on one elbow and blinked at him.

"Spastic," he muttered to himself "Well?"

I cleared my throat. "I, uh, I think I can explain this."

He was hung over and shaking. "Go ahead! Who the devil are you?"

"Well, my name is Dupoir."

"I don't mean what's your name, I mean— Wait a minute. Dupoir?"

"Dupoir."

"As in $14,752.03?"

"That's right, Mr. Bermingham."

"You!" he gasped. "Say, you've got some nerve

coming here this way. I ought to teach you a lesson."

I scrambled to my feet. Mighty thews rippling, I tossed back my head and bellowed the death challenge of the giant anthropoids with whom I had been raised.

Bermingham misunderstood. It probably didn't sound like a death challenge to him. He said anxiously, "If you're going to be sick, go in there and do it. Then we're going to straighten this thing out."

I followed his pointing finger. There on one side of the foyer was the door marked *Staff Washroom,* and on the other the door to the street through which I had carried him. It was only the work of a second to decide which to take. I was out the door, down the steps, around the corner and hailing a fortuitous cab before he could react.

By the time I got to the house that Mr. Klaw wanted so badly to take away from us it was 7:40 on my watch. There was no chance at all that Shirl would still be asleep. There was not any very big chance that she had got to sleep at all that night, not with her faithful husband for the first time in the four years of our marriage staying out all night without warning, but no chance at all that she would be still in bed. So there would be explaining to do. Nevertheless I insinuated my key into the lock of the back door, eased it open, slipped ghost-like through and gently closed it behind me.

I smelled like a distillery, I noticed, but my keen, jungle-trained senses brought me no other message. No one was in sight or sound. Not even Butchie was either chattering or weeping to disturb the silence.

I slid silently through the mud-room into the half-bath where I kept a spare razor. I spent five minutes trying to convert myself into the image of a prosperous young executive getting ready to be half an hour late at work, but it was no easy job. There was nothing but soap to shave with, and Butchie had knocked it into the sink. What was left was a blob of jelly, sculpted into a crescent where the dripping tap had eroded it away. Still, I got clean, more or less, and shaved, less.

I entered the kitchen, and then realized that my jungle-trained senses had failed to note the presence of a pot of fresh coffee perking on the stove. I could hear it plainly enough. Smelling it was more difficult; its scent was drowned by the aroma of cheap booze that hung in the air all around me.

So I turned around and yes, there was Shirl on the stairway, holding Butchie by one hand like Maureen O'Sullivan walking Cheeta. She wore an expression of unrelieved tragedy.

It was clearly necessary to give her an explanation at once, whether I had one or not. "Honey," I said, "I'm *sorry*. I met this fellow I hadn't seen in a long time, and we got to talking. I know we should have called. But by the time I realized the time it was so late I was afraid I'd wake you up."

"You can't wear that shirt to the office," she said woefully. "I ironed your blue and gray one with the white cuffs. It's in the closet."

I paused to analyze the situation. It appeared she wasn't angry at all, only upset—which, as any husband of our years knows, is 14,752.03 times worse. In spite of the fact that the reek of booze was making me giddy and fruit flies were buzzing around Shirl's normally immaculate kitchen, I knew what I had to do. "Shirl," I said, falling to one knee, "I apologize."

That seemed to divert her. "Apologize? For what?"

"For staying out all night."

"But you explained all that. You met this fellow you hadn't seen in a long time, and you got to talking. By the time you realized the time it was so late you were afraid you'd wake me up."

"Oh, Shirl," I cried, leaping to my feet and crushing her in my mighty thews. I would have kissed her, but the reek of stale liquor seemed even stronger. I was afraid of what close contact might do, not to mention its effect on Butchie, staring up at me with a thumb and two fingers in his mouth. We Dupoirs never do anything by halves.

But there was a tear in her eye. She said, "I watched Butchie, honestly I did. I always do. When he broke the studio lamp I was watching every minute, remember? He was just too fast for me."

I didn't have any idea what she was talking about. That is not an unfamiliar situation in our house, and I have developed a technique for dealing with it. "What?" I asked.

"He was too fast for me," Shirl said woefully. "When he dumped his vitamins into his raisins and oatmeal I was right there. I went to get some paper napkins, and that was when he did it. But how could I know it would ruin the plastics bin?"

I went into Phase Two. "What plastics bin?"

"*Our* plastics bin." She pointed. "Where Butchie threw the stuff."

At once I saw what she meant. There was a row of four plastic popup recycling bins in our kitchen, one for paper, one for plastics, one for glass and one for metals. They were a credit to us, and to Mr. Horgan and to the Fourteenth Floor. However, the one marked "plastics" was not a credit to anyone any more. It had sprung a leak. A colorless fluid was oozing out of the bottom of it and, whatever it was, it was deeply pitting the floor tiles.

I bent closer and realized where the reek of stale booze was coming from: out of the juices that were seeping from our plastics bin.

"What the devil?" I asked.

Shirl said thoughtfully, "If vitamins can do that to plastic, what do you suppose they do to Butchie's insides?"

"It isn't the vitamins. I know that much." I reached in and hooked the handle of what had been a milk jug, gallon size. It was high-density polythene and about 400 percent more indestructible than Mount Rushmore. It was exactly the kind of plastic jug that people who loved buzzards better than babies have been complaining about finding bobbing around the surf of their favorite bathing beaches, all the world over.

Indestructible or not, it was about 90 percent destroyed. What I pulled out was a handle and part of a neck. The rest drizzled off into a substance very like the stuff I had shaved with. Only that was soap, which one expects to dissolve from time to time. High-density polythene one does not.

The fruit flies were buzzing around me, and everything was very confusing. I was hardly aware that the front doorbell had rung until I noticed that Shirl had gone to answer it.

What made me fully aware of this was Mr. Bermingham's triumphant roar: "Thought I'd find you here, Dupoir! And who are these people—your confederates?"

Bermingham had no terrors for me. I was past that point. I said, "Hello, Mr. Bermingham. This confederate is my wife, the littler one here is my son. Shirl, Butchie—Mr. Bermingham. Mr. Bermingham's the one who is going to take away our house."

Shirl said politely, "You must be tired, Mr. Bermingham. I'll get you a cup of coffee."

Garigolli to Home Base
Chief,
I admit it, we've excreted this one out beyond redemption. Don't bother to reply to this. Just write us off.

I could say that it wasn't entirely the fault of the crew members who stayed behind in the Host's domicile. They thought they had figured out a way to meet Directive Two. They modified some organisms—didn't even use bacteria, just an enzyme that hydrated polythene into what they had every reason to believe was a standard food substance, since the Host had been observed to ingest it with some frequency. There is no wrong-doing there, Chief. Alcohols are standard foods for many organic beings, as you know. And a gift of food has been held to satisfy the second Directive. And add to that they were half out of their plexuses with empathy deprivation.

Nevertheless I admit the gift failed in a fairly basic way, since it seems to have damaged artifacts the Hosts hold valuable.

So I accept the responsibility, Chief. Wipe this expedition off the records. We've failed, and we'll never see our home breeding-slings again.

Please notify our descendants and former co-parents and, if you can, try to let them think we died heroically, won't you?

Garigolli

Shirl has defeated the wrath of far more complex creatures than Mr. Bermingham by offering them coffee—me, for instance. While she got him the clean cup and the spoon and the milk out of the pitcher in the refrigerator, I had time to think.

Mr. Horgan would be interested in what had happened to our plastics Econ-Bin. Not only Mr. Horgan. The Fourteenth Floor would be interested. The ecology freaks themselves would be interested, and maybe would forget about liking buzzards better than babies long enough to say a good word for International Plastics Co.

I mean, this was *significant*. It was big, by which I mean it wasn't little. It was a sort of whole new horizon for plastics. The thing about plastics, as everyone knows, is that once you convert them into trash they *stay* trash. Bury a maple syrup jug in your back yard and five thousand years from now some descendant operating a radar-controlled peony-planter from his back porch will grub it up as shiny as new. But the gunk in our eco-bin was making these plastics, or at least the polythene parts of them, bio-degradable.

What was the gunk? I had no idea. Some random chemical combination between Butchie's oatmeal and his vitamins? I didn't care. It was there, and it worked. If we could isolate the stuff, I had no doubt that the world-famous scientists who gave us the plastic storm window and the popup Eco-Bin could duplicate it. And if we could duplicate it we could sell it to hard-pressed garbagemen all over the world. The Fourteenth Floor would be very pleased.

With me to think was ever to act. I rinsed out one of Butchie's baby-food jars in the sink, scraped some of the stickiest parts of the melting plastic into it and capped it tightly. I couldn't wait to get it to the office.

Mr. Bermingham was staring at me with his mouth open. "Good Lord," he muttered, "playing with filth at his age. What psychic damage we wreak with bad early toilet training."

I had lost interest in Mr. Bermingham. I stood up and told him, "I've got to go to work. I'd be happy to walk you as far as the bus."

"You aren't going anywhere, Dupoir! Came here to talk to you. Going to do it, too. Behavior was absolutely inexcusable, and I demand— Say, Dupoir, you don't have a drink anywhere about the house, do you?"

"More coffee, Mr. Bermingham?" Shirl said politely. "I'm afraid we don't have anything stronger to offer you. We don't keep alcoholic beverages here, or at least not very long. Mr. Dupoir drinks them."

"Thought so," snarled Bermingham. "Recognize a drunk when I see one: shifty eyes, irrational behavior, duplicity—oh, the duplicity! Got all the signs."

"Oh, he's not like my brother, really," Shirl said thoughtfully. "My husband doesn't go out breaking into liquor stores when he runs out, you know. But I don't drink, and Butchie doesn't drink, and so about all we ever have in the house is some cans of beer, and there aren't any of those now."

Bermingham looked at her with angry disbelief. "You too! I *smell* it," he said. "You going to tell me

I don't know what good old ethyl alcohol smells like?"

"That's the bin, Mr. Bermingham. It's a terrible mess, I know."

"Funny place to keep the creature," he muttered to himself, dropping to his knees. He dipped a finger into the drippings, smelled it, tasted it and nodded. "Alcohol, all right. Add a few congeners, couple drops of food coloring, and you've got the finest Chivas Regal a bellboy ever sold you out of a bottle with the tax stamp broken." He stood up and glared at me. "What's the matter with you, Dupoir? You not only don't pay your honest debts, you don't want to pay the bartenders either?"

I said, "It's more or less an accident."

"Accident?"

Then illumination struck. "Accident you should find us like this," I corrected. "You see, it's a secret new process. We're not ready to announce it yet. Making alcohol out of old plastic scraps."

He questioned Shirl with his eyes. Getting her consent, he poured some of Butchie's baby-food orange juice into a glass, scooped in some of the drippings from the bin, closed his eyes and tasted. "Mmm," he said judiciously. "Sell it for vodka just the way it stands."

"Glad to have an expert opinion," I said. "We think there's millions in it."

He took another taste. "Plastic scraps, you say? Listen, Dupoir. Think we can clear all this up in no time. That fool Klaw, I've told him over and over, ask politely, don't make trouble for people. But no, he's got that crazy lawyer's drive for revenge. Apologize for him, old boy, I really do apologize for him. Now look," he said, putting down the glass to rub his hands. "You'll need help in putting this process on the market. Business acumen, you know? Wise counsel from man of experience. Like me. And capital. Can help you there. I'm loaded."

Shirl put in, "Then what do you want our house for?"

"House? My dear Mrs. Dupoir," cried Mr. Bermingham, laughing heartily, "I'm not going to take your house! Your husband and I will work out the details in no time. Let me have a little more of that delightful orange juice and we can talk some business."

Garigolli to Home Base
Joy, joy
Chief!
Cancel all I said. We've met Directive Two, the Host is happy, and we're on our way Home!
Warm up the breeding slings, there's going to be a hot time in the old hammocks tonight.

Garigolli

Straight as the flight of Ung-Glitch, the soaring vulture, that is the code of the jungle. I was straight with Mr. Bermingham. I didn't cheat him. I made a handshake deal with him over the ruins of our Eco-Bin, and honored it when we got to his lawyers. I traded him 40 percent of the beverage rights to the stuff that came out of our bin, and he wrote off that little matter of $14,752.03.

Of course, the beverage rights turned out not to be worth all that much, because the stuff in the bin was organic and alive and capable of reproduction, and it did indeed reproduce itself enthusiastically. Six months later you could buy a starter drop of it for a quarter on any street corner, and what that has done to the vintners of the world you know as well as I do. But Bermingham came out ahead. He divided his 40 percent interest into forty parts and sold them for $500 each to the alumni of his drunk tank. And Mr. Horgan—

Ah, Mr. Horgan.

Mr. Horgan was perched on my doorframe like Ung-Glitch awaiting a delivery of cadavers for dinner when I arrived that morning, bearing my little glass jar before me like the waiting line in an obstetrician's office. "You're late, Dupoir," he pointed out. "Troubles me, that does. Do you remember Metcalf? Tall, blonde girl that used to work in Accounts Receivable? Never could get in on time, and—"

"Mr. Horgan," I said, "look." And I unscrewed my baby-food jar and dumped the contents on an unpopped pop-up Eco-Bin. It took him a while to see what was happening, but once he saw he was so impressed he forgot to roar.

And, yes, the Fourteenth Floor was very pleased.

There wasn't any big money in it. We couldn't sell the stuff, because it was so happy to give itself away to everyone in the world. But it meant a promotion and a raise. Not big. But not really little, either. And, as Mr. Horgan said, "I *like* the idea of helping to eliminate all the litter that devastates the landscape. It makes me feel, I don't know, like part of something clean and natural."

And so we got along happily as anything—happily, anyway, until the time Shirl bought the merry-go-round.

A GENTLE DYING

This was actually to have been the first story Cyril and I collaborated on; in fact, even before that, it was to have been my own first novel. When I first began writing professionally I conceived the notion of a science-fiction novel to be entitled *Sex Dream of a Precocious Twelve-Year-Old.* I am no longer sure of what it was to be about, except that it had something to do with everyone's dreams of flying, and something to do with the dying fantasies of a child. I told Cyril about it, he volunteered to collaborate, he went home and produced a first chapter and we lost it. When it turned up again, after his death, I had long since forgotten whatever it was I intended for the novel, but I saw a short story in it . . . and this is it.

ELPHEN DeBeckett lay dying. It was time. He had lived in the world for one hundred and nine years, though he had seen little enough of it except for the children. The children, thank God, still came. He thought they were with him now: "Coppie," he whispered in a shriveled voice, "how nice to see you." The nurse did not look around, although she was the only person in the room besides himself, and knew that he was not addressing her.

The nurse was preparing the injections the doctor had ordered her to have ready. This little capsule for shock, this to rally his strength, these half-dozen others to shield him from his pain. Most of them would be

83

used. DeBeckett was dying in a pain that once would
have been unbearable and even now caused him to
thresh about sometimes and moan.

DeBeckett's room was a great twelve-foot chamber with hanging drapes and murals that reflected
scenes from his books. The man himself was tiny,
gnomelike. He became even less material while death
(prosey biology, the chemistry of colloids) drew in-
appropriately near his head. He had lived his life remote from everything a normal man surrounds himself
with. He now seemed hardly alive enough to die.

DeBeckett lay in a vast, pillared bed, all the vaster
for the small burden he put on it, and the white linen
was whiter for his merry brown face. "Darling Ved-
die, please don't cry," he whispered restlessly, and the
nurse took up a hypodermic syringe. He was not in
unusual pain, though, and she put it back and sat down
beside him.

The world had been gentle with the gentle old
man. It had made him a present of this bed and this
linen, this great house with its attendant horde of machines to feed and warm and comfort him, and the
land on which stood the tiny, quaint houses he loved
better. It had given him a park in the mountains, well
stocked with lambs, deer and birds of blazing, spec-
tacular color, a fenced park where no one ever went
but DeBeckett and the beloved children, where earth-
moving machines had scooped out a Very Own Pond
("My Very Own Pond/Which I sing for you in this
song/Is eight Hippopotamuses Wide/And twenty Ele-
phants long.") He had not seen it for years, but he
knew it was there. The world had given him, most of
all, money, more money than he could ever want. He
had tried to give it back (gently, hopefully, in a way
pathetically), but there was always more. Even now
the world showered him with gifts and doctors, though
neither could prevail against the stomping pitchfire ar-
sonist in the old man's colon. The disease, a form of
gastroenteritis, could have been cured; medicine had

come that far long since. But not in a body that clung so lightly to life.

He opened his eyes and said strongly, "Nurse, are the children there?"

The nurse was a woman of nearly sixty. That was why she had been chosen. The new medicine was utterly beyond her in theory, but she could follow directions; and she loved Elphen DeBeckett. Her love was the love of a child, for a thumbed edition of *Coppie Brambles* had brightened her infancy. She said, "Of course they are, Mr. DeBeckett."

He smiled. The old man loved children very much. They had been his whole life. The hardest part of his dying was that nothing of his own flesh would be left, no son, no grandchild, no one. He had never married. He would have given almost anything to have a child of his blood with him now—almost anything, except the lurid, grunting price nature exacts, for De-Beckett had never known a woman. His only children were the phantoms of his books . . . and those who came to visit him. He said faintly, "Let the little sweetlings in."

The nurse slipped out and the door closed silently behind her. Six children and three adults waited patiently outside, DeBeckett's doctor among them. Quickly she gave him the dimensions of the old man's illness, pulse and temperature, and the readings of the tiny gleaming dials by his pillow as well, though she did not know what they measured. It did not matter. She knew what the doctor was going to say before he said it: "He can't last another hour. It is astonishing that he lasted this long," he added, "but we will have lost something when he goes."

"He wants you to come in. Especially you—" She glanced around, embarrassed. "Especially you children." She had almost said "little sweetlings" herself, but did not quite dare. Only Elphen DeBeckett could talk like that, even to children. Especially to children.

Especially to these children, poised, calm, beautiful, strong and gay. Only the prettiest, sweetest children visited Elphen DeBeckett, half a dozen or a score every day, a year-in, year-out pilgrimage. He would not have noticed if they had been ugly and dull, of course. To DeBeckett all children were sweet, beautiful and bright.

They entered and ranged themselves around the bed, and DeBeckett looked up. The eyes regarded them and a dying voice said, "Please read to me," with such resolute sweetness that it frightened. "From my book," it added, though they knew well enough what he meant.

The children looked at each other. They ranged from four to eleven, Will, Mike, blonde Celine, brown-eyed Karen, fat Freddy and busy Pat. "You," said Pat, who was seven.

"No," said five-year-old Freddy. "Will."

"Celine," said Will. "Here."

The girl named Celine took the book from him and began obediently. " 'Coppie thought to herself—' "

"No," said Pat. "Open."

The girl opened the book, embarrassed, glancing at the dying old man. He was smiling at her without amusement, only love. She began to read:

Coppie thought to herself that the geese might be hungry, for she herself ate Lotsandlots. Mumsie often said so, though Coppie had never found out what that mysterious food might be. She could not find any, so took some bread from Brigid Marie Ann-Erica Evangeline, the Cook Whose Name Was So Long That She Couldn't Remember It All Herself. As she walked along Dusty Path to Coppie Brambles's Very Own Pond—

Celine hesitated, looking at the old man with sharp worry, for he had moaned faintly, like a flower moaning. "No, love," he said. "Go on." The swelling soft bubble before his heart had turned on him, but he knew he still had time.

The little girl read:

—As she walked along Dusty Path to Coppie Brambles's Very Own Pond, she thought and thought, and what she thought finally came right out of her mouth. It was a Real Gay Think, to be Thought While Charitably Feeding Geese:
They don't make noise like little girls and boys,
And all day long they're aswimming.
They never fret and sputter 'cause they haven't any butter,
They go where the water's wetly brimming.
But say—
Anyway—
I
Like
Geese!

There was more, but the child paused and, after a moment, closed the book. DeBeckett was no longer listening. He was whispering to himself.

On the wall before him was painted a copy of one of the illustrations from the first edition of his book, a delightful picture of Coppie Brambles herself, feeding the geese, admirably showing her shyness and her trace of fear, contrasted with the loutish comedy of the geese. The old man's eyes were fixed on the picture as he whispered. They guessed he was talking to Coppie, the child of eight dressed in the fashions of eighty years ago. They could hardly hear him, but in the silence that fell on the room his voice grew stronger.

He was saying, without joy but without regret. "No more meadows, no more of the laughter of little children. But I do love them." He opened his eyes and sat up, waving the nurse away. "No, my dear," he said cheerfully, "it does not matter if I sit up now, you know. Excuse me for my rudeness. Excuse an old and tired man who, for a moment, wished to live on. I have something to say to you all."

The nurse, catching a sign from the doctor, took up another hypodermic and made it ready. "Please, Mr. DeBeckett," she said. Good humored, he permitted her to spray the surface of his wrist with a fine mist of droplets that touched the skin and penetrated it. "I suppose that is to give me strength," he said. "Well, I am grateful for it. I know I must leave you, but there is something I would like to know. I have wondered . . . For years I have wondered, but I have not been able to understand the answers when I was told them. I think I have only this one more chance."

He felt stronger from the fluid that now coursed through his veins, and accepted without fear the price he would have to pay for it. "As you know," he said, "or, I should say, as you children no doubt do not know, some years ago I endowed a research institution, the Coppie Brambles Foundation. I did it for the love of you, you and all of you. Last night I was reading the letter I wrote my attorneys—No. Let us see if you can understand the letter itself; I have it here. Will, can you read?"

Will was nine, freckled darkly on pale skin, red haired and gangling. "Yes, Mr. DeBeckett."

"Even hard words," smiled the dying man.

"Yes, sir."

DeBeckett gestured at the table beside him, and the boy obediently took up a stiff sheet of paper. "Please," said DeBeckett, and the boy began to read in a highpitched, rapid whine.

" 'Children have been all my life and I have not regretted an instant of the years I devoted to their happiness. If I can tell them a little of the wonderful world in which we are, if I can open to them the miracles of life and living, then my joy is unbounded. This I have tried, rather selfishly, to do. I cannot say it was for them! It was for me. For nothing could have given me more pleasure.' "

The boy paused.

DeBeckett said gravely, "I'm afraid this is a Very Big Think, lovelings. Please try to understand. This is the letter I wrote to my attorneys when I instructed them to set up the Foundation. Go on, Will."

" 'But my way of working has been unscientific, I know. I am told that children are not less than we adults, but more. I am told that the grown-up maimers and cheats in the world are only children soiled, that the hagglers of commerce are the infant dreamers whose dreams were denied. I am told that youth is wilder, freer, better than age, which I believe with all my heart, not needing the stories of twenty-year-old mathematicians and infant Mozarts to lay a proof.

" 'In the course of my work I have been given great material rewards. I wish that this money be spent for those I love. I have worked with the heart, but perhaps my money can help someone to work with the mind, in this great new science of psychology which I do not understand, in all of the other sciences which I understand even less. I must hire other eyes.

" 'I direct, then, that all of my assets other than my books and my homes be converted into cash, and that this money be used to further the study of the child, with the aim of releasing him from the corrupt adult cloak that smothers him, of freeing him for wisdom, tenderness and love.' "

"That," said DeBeckett sadly, "was forty years ago."

He started at a sound. Overhead a rocket was clapping through the sky, and DeBeckett looked wildly around. "It's all right, Mr. DeBeckett," comforted little Pat. "It's only a plane."

He allowed her to soothe him. "Ah, loveling," he said. "And can you answer my question?"

"What it says in the 'Cyclopedia, Mr. DeBeckett?"

"Why— Yes, if you know it, my dear."

Surprisingly the child said, as if by rote: "The Institute was founded in 1976 and at once attracted most of the great workers in pediatric analysis, who were able to show Wiltshanes's Effect in the relationship between glandular and mental development. Within less than ten years a new projective analysis of the growth process permitted a reorientation of basic pedagogy from a null-positive locus. The effects were immediate. The first generation of—"

She stopped, startled. The old man was up on his elbow, his eyes blazing at her in wonder and fright. "I'm—" She looked around at the other children for help and at once wailed, "I'm *sorry*, Mr. DeBeckett!" and began to cry.

The old man fell back, staring at her with a sort of unbelieving panic. The little girl wept abundantly. Slowly DeBeckett's expression relaxed and he managed a sketchy smile.

He said, "There, sweetest. You startled me. But it was charming of you to memorize all that!"

"I learned it for you," she sobbed.

"I didn't understand. Don't cry." Obediently the little girl dried her eyes as DeBeckett stretched out a hand to her.

But the hand dropped back on the quilt. Age, surprise and the drug had allied to overmaster the dwindling resources of Elphen DeBeckett. He wandered to the plantoms on the wall. "I never understood what they did with my money," he told Coppie, who smiled at him with a shy, painted smile. "The children kept coming, but they never said."

"Poor man," said Will absently, watching him with a child's uncommitted look.

The nurse's eyes were bright and wet. She reached for the hypodermic, but the doctor shook his head.

"Wait," he said, and walked to the bed. He stood on tiptoe to peer into the dying man's face. "No, no use. Too old. Can't survive organ transplant, certainty of cytic shock. No feasible therapy." The nurse's eyes were now flowing. The doctor said to her, with patience but not very much patience, "No alternative. Only kept him going this long from gratitude."

The nurse sobbed, "Isn't there *anything* we can do for him?"

"Yes." The doctor gestured, and the lights on the diagnostic dials winked out. "We can let him die."

Little Pat hiked herself up on a chair, much too large for her, and dangled her feet. "Be nice to get rid of this furniture, anyway," she said. "Well, nurse? He's dead. Don't wait." The nurse looked rebelliously at the doctor, but the doctor only nodded. Sadly the nurse went to the door and admitted the adults who had waited outside. The four of them surrounded the body and bore it gently through the door. Before it closed the nurse looked back and wailed: "He loved you!"

The children did not appear to notice. After a moment Pat said reflectively, "Sorry about the book. Should have opened it."

"He didn't notice," said Will, wiping his hands. He had touched the old man's fingers.

"No. Hate crying, though."

The doctor said, "Nice of you. Helped him, I think." He picked up the phone and ordered a demolition crew for the house. "Monument?"

"Oh, yes," said another child. "Well. Small one, anyway."

The doctor, who was nine, said, "Funny. Without him, what? A few hundred thousand dollars and the Foundation makes a flexible world, no more rigid adults, no more—" He caught himself narrowly. The doctor had observed before that he had a tendency to over-identify with adults, probably because his specialty had been geriatrics. Now that Elphen DeBeckett was dead, he no longer had a specialty.

"Miss him somehow," said Celine frankly, coming over to look over Will's shoulder at the quaint old murals on the wall. "What the nurse said, true enough. He loved us."

"And clearly we loved him," piped Freddy, methodically sorting through the contents of the dead man's desk. "Would have terminated him with the others otherwise, wouldn't we?"

A HINT OF HENBANE

This is unlike the other stories in this volume in two respects. First, it isn't science fiction. Second, it wasn't left as an incomplete fragment. It was a finished story, which had somehow gone sour, and never sold. I thought I could see why, so I put it through the typewriter again, and gave it to Bob Mills as agent, and it was published at once in *Alfred Hitchcock's Mystery Magazine*.

I USED TO THINK, not that it bothered me, that my wife systematically lied to me about her family, but one by one I met them and found it was all true. There was Uncle H_____, for one. He earned his unprintable nickname on the day in 1937 when he said to the bank examiner, "Oh, h_____!", walked right down to the depot and got on a westbound train, never to return. He sounded like a wish-fulfillment myth, but two summers ago we drove through Colorado and looked him up. Uncle H_____ was doing fine; brown as a berry, and gave us bear ham out of his own smokehouse for lunch. And, just the way the story went, his shanty was papered with color comics from the Chicago Sunday *Tribune*.

Uncle Edgar, the salesman, was real too. Sarah claimed that in 1942 he had sold a Wisconsin town on turning over its municipal building to him so he could start a war plant. Well, last year I visited him in his executive suite, which used to be the mayor's office. He had converted to roller skates. Whenever anyone hinted to him that he might start paying rent or taxes or something he would murmur quietly that he was thinking of moving plant and payroll to Puerto Rico, and then there would be no more hinting for a while.

Grandma and Grandpa were right off the cover of the *Saturday Evening Post,* rocking and dozing on the porch of their big house. Grandpa, if pressed, would modestly display his bullet scars from the Oklahoma land rush, and Sarah assured me that Grandma had some too. *Great* Grandmother, pushing the century mark a couple miles down the road, gloomily queened it over five hundred central Ohio acres from her dusty plush bedroom. She had decided in '35 that she would go to bed, and stuck to this decision while suburban housing developments and shopping centers and drive-in movies encroached on the old farm, and the money rolled in. Sarah had a grudging respect for her, though she had seen the will, and it was all going to a Baptist mission in Naples, Italy.

There was even at last a strained sort of peace between Sarah and her father. He came out of World War I with a D.S.C., a silver plate in his skull and a warped outlook on civilian life. He was a bootlegger throughout most of the twenties. It made for an unpleasant childhood. When it was too late to do the children much good, the V.A. replaced his silver plate with a tantalum plate and he promptly enrolled in a theological seminary and wound up a Lutheran pastor in southern California.

Sarah's attitude toward all this is partly "Judge not lest ye be judged" and partly "What the hell," but of her cousin's husband, Bill Oestreicher, she said dogmatically: "He's a lousy bastard."

We used to see more of him than of the rest of her family, as an unavoidable side effect of visiting Sarah's Cousin Claire, to whom he was married. Sarah was under some special indebtedness to Cousin Claire.

I think Claire used to take her in during the rough spells with Dad.

On the way to meet them for the first time—they lived in Indiana, an easy drive from Detroit—Sarah told me: "Try to enjoy the scenery, because you won't enjoy Bill. Did I say you weren't to lend him money or go into any kind of business deal with him?"

"You did."

"And one other thing, don't talk to him about your own business. Uncle Edgar let him mail a couple of customers' statements for him, and Bill went to the customers offering to undercut Edgar's prices. There was hell's own confusion for a month, and Edgar lost two customers to the Japs. To this day Bill can't understand why Edgar won't talk to him any more."

"I will come out fighting and protect my chin at all times."

"You'd better."

Claire was a dark, bird-like little woman with an eager-to-please air, very happy to see Sarah and willing to let some of it splash over onto me. She had just come from work. She was a city visiting nurse and wore a snappy blue cape and hat. Even after eight hours of helping a nineteen-year-old girl fight D.T.'s, she was neat, every hair in place. I suspected a compulsion. She wore a large, incongruous costume-jewelry sort of ring which I concluded to be a dime-store anniversary present from good old Bill.

Bill's first words to me were: "Glad to meet you, Tommy. Tommy, how much money can you raise in a pinch?" I came out fighting. I've got an automotive upholstery business with a few good accounts. The Ford buyer could ruin me overnight by drawing a line through my name on his list, but until that happens I'm solvent. I concealed this from Bill. It was easy. At fifty-odd he was a fat infant. He was sucking on candy sourballs, and when he crunched them up he opened a box of Cracker Jacks. I never saw him when he wasn't munching, gulping, sucking. Beer, gum, chocolates, pretzels—he was the only person I ever heard of who *lapped* pretzels—pencils, the ear pieces of his horn-rimmed glasses, the ends of his moustache. Slop, slurp, slop. With his mouth open.

Bill maneuvered me into the kitchen, sucked on a quartered orange and told me he was going to let me in on a can't-miss scrap syndicate which would buy Army surplus and sell it right back to the government at full price. I told him no he wasn't.

His surprise was perfectly genuine. "What do you want to be like that for?" he asked, round-eyed, and went over it again with pencil and paper, sucking on the end of the pencil when he wasn't scribbling with it, and when I said no again he got angry.

"Tommy, what're you being so stupid for? Can't you see I'm just trying to give one of Claire's people a helping hand? Now *listen* this time, I haven't got all day." My God, what can you do? I told him I'd think about it.

He shook my hand. Between chomps and slurps he said it was a wise decision; if I could pony up, say, five thousand we'd get underway with a rush; had I thought of a second mortgage on my house? "Let's celebrate it," he said. "Claire. *Claire,* Goddamn it!"

She popped in. "Case of beer," he said. He didn't even look at her. "The beauty of this, Tommy, is it's Air Force money. Who's going to say no when the Air Force wants to buy something. Tommy, what about borrowing on your insurance?"

Cousin Claire came staggering up from the basement with a case of twenty-four bottles of beer. "Nice and cold," she panted. "From the north corner."

He said, "Giddadahere. Now the markup—" She fluttered out. He turned to the case of beer, and his eyes popped. "How do you like that?" he asked me incredulously. "She didn't open any. She must have thought I wanted to *look* at beer."

"Well," I said, "you know." Martyred, he got a bottle opener from a drawer.

Driving back to Detroit I was in a state of shock for about twenty miles. Finally I was able to ask Sarah: *"Why* in God's name did she marry him?"

She said hopelessly: "I think it's because they won't let you be an old maid any more. She got middle-aged, she got panicky, Bill turned up and they were married. He gets a job once in a while. His people are in politics. . . . She's still got her ring," Sarah said with pride.

"Huh?"

"The Charlier ring. Topaz signet—didn't you see it?"

"What about it?"

"Bill's been trying to get it away from her ever since they were married, but *I'm* going to get it next. It's family. It's a big topaz, and it swivels. One side is plain, and the other side has the Charlier crest, and it's a poison ring."

I honked at a convertible that was about to pull out in front and kill us. "You'll hate me for this," I said, "but there aren't any poison rings. There never were."

"Nuts to you," she said, indignant. "I've opened it with my own little fingers. It comes apart in two little slices of topaz, and there's a hollow for the poison."

"Not poison. Maybe a saint's relic, or a ladylike pinch of snuff. In the olden days they didn't have poisons that fitted into little hollows. You had to use *quarts* of what they had. Everything you've heard to the contrary is bunk because everybody used to think everybody else had powerful, subtle poisons. Now, of course, we've got all kinds of—"

She wasn't listening. "Somebody unwisely told Bill that the Ford Museum offered my grandmother a thousand dollars for the ring. Ever since then he's been after her to sell it so he can 'put the money into a business.' But she won't. . . . She doesn't look well, Tommy." I spared a second from the traffic to glance at her. There were tears in her eyes.

A week later began a series of semiliterate, petulant letters from Cousin Bill.

He was, or said he was, under the impression that I had pledged my sacred word of honor to put up $30,000 and go in with him on the junk deal. I answered the first letter, trying to set him straight, and ignored the rest when I realized he couldn't be set straight. Not by me, not by anybody. The world was what he wanted it to be. If it failed him, he screamed and yelled at the world until it got back into line.

We saw them a couple of months later. He bore me no malice. He tried to get me to back a chain of filling stations whose gimmick would be a special brand of oil—filtered crankcase drainings, picked up for a song, dyed orange and handsomely packaged. He took to using my company name as a credit reference, and I had my lawyer write him a letter, after which he took to using my lawyer's name as a credit reference. We saw him again, and he still was not angry. Munching and slobbering and prying, he just didn't understand how I could be so stupid as not to realize that he wanted to help me. At every visit he was fat, and Claire was thinner.

He complained about it. Licking the drips off the side of an ice cream cone he said: "By God you ought to have more meat on your bones. The way the grocery bills run."

"Has it ever occurred to you," Sarah snapped, "that your wife might be a sick woman?"

Cousin Claire made shushing noises. Cousin Bill chewed the cone, looking at her. "No kidding," he said, licking his finger. "For God's sake, Claire. We got Blue Cross, Blue Shield, City Health, we been paying all these years, won't cost a nickel. What's the matter with you? You go get a checkup."

"I'll be all right," said Cousin Claire, buttering a slice of pound cake for her husband.

Afterward I burst out: "All right, I'm not a doctor, I supply auto upholstery fabrics, but can't you get her to a hospital?"

Sarah was very calm. "I understand now. She knows what she's doing. In Claire's position—what would you do?"

I thought it over and said, "Oh," and after that drove very carefully. It occurred to me that we had something to live for, and that Cousin Claire had not.

My wife phoned me at the office a few weeks later, and she was crying. "The mail's just come. A letter from a nurse, friend of Claire's. Bill's put her in the hospital."

"Well, Sarah, I mean, isn't that where she ought to—"

"No!" So that night we drove to Indiana and went direct to Claire's hospital room—her one-seventh of a room, that is. Bill had put her in a ward. But she was already dead.

We drove to their house, ostensibly to get a burial dress for Cousin Claire, perhaps really to knock Cousin Bill down and jump on his face. Sarah had seen the body, and neither on the clawed finger nor in the poor effects I checked out at the desk was the ring. "He took it," Sarah said. "I know. Because she was three weeks dying, the floor nurse told me. And Claire told me she knew it was coming, and she had hyoscine in the ring." So Sarah had her triumph after all, and the ring had become a poison ring, for a sick, despairing woman's quick way out of disappointment and pain. "The lousy bastard," Sarah said. "Tommy. I want her buried with the ring."

I felt her trembling. Well, so was I. He had taken the ring from a woman too sick to protect herself and for the sake of a thousand lousy bucks he had cheated her of her exit. I don't mean that. I'm a businessman. There is nothing lousy about a thousand bucks, but . . . I wanted to bury her with the ring too.

No one answered the front door, and when we went around to the pantry and found it open we found out why. Bill was slumped in a kitchen chair facing us, a spilled bottle of beer tacky on the linoleum, a bag of pretzels open in front of him and his finger in his mouth. You know what hyoscine is? They used to get it from henbane before they learned to put it together in a test tube more cheaply. It was a good, well-considered substance for a nurse to put in her ring because it kills like *that*. Slobbering infant, Bill must not have been able to resist taking the ring from her. And then he could not resist putting it in his mouth.

THE MEETING

A few years before his death, Cyril wrote a story
about a school for "exceptional" children. It was not
science fiction; it was not exactly a story, for that
matter (being more description than event) and no
one seemed to want to buy it. But it came out of
Cyril's heart, because one of his children was in just
such a school. After his death I found the manuscript
(or what was left of it, a page or two being missing)
and it reached my heart as well. For the same reason.
It lay in my files for years until I happened to come
across it while looking for something else, and realized
that it fit in well with a story notion that had been
germinating in my mind, and "The Meeting" came
out. It was awarded a Hugo at the 1973 World Science
Fiction Convention in Toronto. It was my first writing
Hugo (I've had some as an editor) and I was very glad
to get it; but even more glad to be able to send the
duplicate trophy to Cyril's widow, as a long-overdue
tribute to one of the most talented writers who ever
graced our field.

HARRY VLADEK was too large for a man for his Volks-
wagen, but he was too poor a man to trade it in, and
as things were going he was going to stay that way a
long time. He applied the brakes carefully ("Master
cylinder's leaking like a sieve, Mr. Vladek; what's the
use of just fixing up the linings?"—but the estimate
was a hundred and twenty-eight dollars, and where
was it going to come from?) and parked in the neat-

ly graveled lot. He squeezed out of the door, the upsetting telephone call from Dr. Nicholson on his mind,
locked the car up and went into the school building.

The Parent-Teachers Association of the Bing-
ham County School for Exceptional Children was holding its first meeting of the term. Of the twenty people
already there, Vladek knew only Mrs. Adler, the principal, or headmistress, or owner of the school. She was
the one he needed to talk to most, he thought. Would
there be any chance to see her privately? Right now
she sat across the room at her scuffed golden oak desk
in a posture chair, talking in low, rapid tones with a
gray-haired woman in a tan suit. A teacher? She
seemed too old to be a parent, although his wife had
told him some of the kids seemed to be twenty or more.

It was 8:30 and the parents were still driving up
to the school, a converted building that had once been
a big country house—almost a mansion. The living
room was full of elegant reminders of that. *Two* chan-
deliers. Intricate vine-leaf molding on the plaster
above the dropped ceiling. The pink-veined white mar-
ble fireplace, unfortunately prominent because of the
unsuitable andirons, too cheap and too small, that now
stood in it. Golden oak sliding double doors to the
hall. And visible through them a grim, fireproof staircase of concrete and steel. They must, Vladek thought,
have had to rip out a beautiful wooden thing to install
the fireproof stairs for compliance with the state school
laws.

People kept coming in, single men, single women,
and occasionally a couple. He wondered how the cou-
ples managed their baby-sitting problem. The subtitle
on the school's letterhead was "an institution for emotionally disturbed and cerebrally damaged children
capable of education." Harry's nine-year-old Thomas
was one of the emotionally disturbed ones. With a
taste of envy he wondered if cerebrally damaged children could be baby-sat by any reasonably competent

grownup. Thomas could not. The Vladeks had not had an evening out together since he was two, so that tonight Margaret was holding the fort at home, no doubt worrying herself sick about the call from Dr. Nicholson, while Harry was representing the family at the PTA.

As the room filled up, chairs were getting scarce. A young couple was standing at the end of the row near him, looking around for a pair of empty seats. "Here," he said to them. "I'll move over." The woman smiled politely and the man said thanks. Emboldened by an ashtray on the empty seat in front of him, Harry pulled out his pack of cigarettes and offered it to them, but it turned out they were nonsmokers. Harry lit up anyway, listening to what was going on around him.

Everybody was talking. One woman asked another, "How's the gall bladder? Are they going to take it out after all?" A heavy, balding man said to a short man with bushy sideburns, "Well, my accountant says the tuition's medically deductible if the school is for psycho*somatic,* not just for psycho. That we've got to clear up." The short man told him positively, "Right, but all you need is a doctor's letter; he recommends the school, refers the child to the school." And a very young woman said intensely, "Dr. Shields was very optimistic, Mrs. Clerman. He says without a doubt the thyroid will make Georgie accessible. And then—" A light-coffee-colored black man in an aloha shirt told a plump woman, "He really pulled a wing-ding over the weekend, two stitches in his face, busted my fishing pole in three places." And the woman said, "They get so bored. My little girl has this thing about crayons, so that rules out coloring books altogether. You wonder what you can do."

Harry finally said to the young man next to him, "My name's Vladek. I'm Tommy's father; he's in the beginners group."

"That's where ours is," said the young man. "He's Vern. Six years old. Blond like me. Maybe you've seen him."

Harry did not try very hard to remember. The two or three times he had picked Tommy up after class he had not been able to tell one child from another in the great bustle of departure. Coats, handkerchiefs, hats, one little girl who always hid in the supply closet and a little boy who never wanted to go home and hung onto the teacher. "Oh, yes," he said politely.

The young man introduced himself and his wife; they were named Murray and Celia Logan. Harry leaned over the man to shake the wife's hand, and she said, "Aren't you new here?"

"Yes. Tommy's been in the school a month. We moved in from Elmira to be near it." He hesitated, then added, "Tommy's nine, but the reason he's in the beginners group is that Mrs. Adler thought it would make the adjustment easier."

Logan pointed to a suntanned man in the first row. "See that fellow with the glasses? He moved here from *Texas*. Of course, he's got money."

"It must be a good place," Harry said questioningly.

Logan grinned, his expression a little nervous.

"How's your son?" Harry asked.

"That little rascal," said Logan. "Last week I got him another copy of the *My Fair Lady* album, I guess he's used up four or five of them, and he goes around singing 'luv-er-ly, luv-er-ly.' But *look* at you? No."

"Mine doesn't talk," said Harry.

Mrs. Logan said judiciously, "Ours talks. Not *to* anybody, though. It's like a wall."

"I know," said Harry, and pressed. "Has, ah, has Vern shown much improvement with the school?"

Murray Logan pursed his lips. "I would say, yes. The bedwetting's not too good, but life's a great deal smoother in some ways. You know, you don't hope for a dramatic breakthrough. But in little things, day by day, it goes smoother. Mostly smoother. Of course there are setbacks."

Harry nodded, thinking of seven years of setbacks, and two years of growing worry and puzzlement before that. He said, "Mrs. Adler told me that, for instance, a special outbreak of destructiveness might mean something like a plateau in speech therapy. So the child fights it and breaks out in some other direction."

"That too," said Logan, "but what I meant— Oh, they're starting."

Vladek nodded, stubbing out his cigarette and absent-mindedly lighting another. His stomach was knotting up again. He wondered at these other parents, who seemed so safe and, well, untouched. Wasn't it the same with them as with Margaret and himself? And it had been a long time since either of them had felt the world comfortable around them, even without Dr. Nicholson pressing for a decision. He forced himself to lean back and look as tranquil as the others.

Mrs. Adler was tapping her desk with a ruler. "I think everybody who is coming is here," she said. She leaned against the desk and waited for the room to quiet down. She was short, dark, plump and surprisingly pretty. She did not look at all like a competent professional. She looked so unlike her role that, in fact, Harry's heart had sunk three months ago when their correspondence about admitting Tommy had been climaxed by the long trip from Elmira for the interview. He had expected a steel-gray lady with rimless glasses, a Valkyrie in a white smock like the nurse who had held wriggling, screaming Tommy while waiting for the suppository to quiet him down for his first EEG, a disheveled old fraud, he didn't know what. Anything except this pretty young woman. Another blind alley, he had thought in despair. Another, after a hundred too many already. First, "Wait for him to outgrow it." He doesn't. Then, "We must reconcile ourselves to God's will." But you don't want to. Then give him the prescription three times a day for three months. And it doesn't work. Then chase around for six months with the Child Guidance Clinic to find out it's only letterheads and one circuit-riding doctor who doesn't have time for anything. Then, after four dreary, weepy weeks of soul-searching, the State Training School, and find out it has an eight-year waiting list. Then the private custodial school, and find they're fifty-five hundred dollars a year—without medical treatment!—and where do you get fifty-five hundred dollars a year? And all the time everybody warns you, as if you didn't know it: "Hurry! Do something! Catch it early! This is the critical stage! Delay is fatal!" And then this soft-looking little woman; how could she do anything?

She had rapidly shown him how. She had questioned Margaret and Harry incisively, turned to Tommy, rampaging through that same room like a rogue bull, and turned his rampage into a game. In three minutes he was happily experimenting with an indestructible old windup cabinet Victrola, and Mrs. Adler was saying to the Vladeks, "Don't count on a miracle cure. There isn't any. But improvements, yes, and I think we can help Tommy."

Perhaps she had, thought Vladek bleakly. Perhaps she was helping as much as anyone ever could.

Meanwhile Mrs. Adler had quickly and pleasantly welcomed the parents, suggested they remain for coffee and get to know each other, and introduced the PTA president, a Mrs. Rose, tall, prematurely gray and very executive. "This being the first meeting of the term," she said, "there are no minutes to be read; so we'll get to the committee work reports. What about the transportation problem, Mr. Baer?"

The man who got up was old. More than sixty; Harry wondered what it was like to have your life crowned with a late retarded child. He wore all the trappings of success—a four-hundred-dollar suit, an electronic wrist watch, a large gold fraternal ring. In a slight German accent he said, "I was to the district school board and they are not cooperating. My lawyer looked it up and the trouble is all one word. What the law says, the school board may, that is the word, may reimburse parents of handicapped children for transportation to private schools. Not shall, you understand, but may. They were very frank with me. They said they just didn't want to spend the money. They have the impression we're all rich people here."

Slight sour laughter around the room.

"So my lawyer made an appointment, and we appeared before the full board and presented the case —we don't care, reimbursement, a school bus, anything so we can relieve the transportation burden a little. The answer was no." He shrugged and remained standing, looking at Mrs. Rose, who said:

"Thank you, Mr. Baer. Does anybody have any suggestions?"

A woman said angrily, "Put some heat on them. We're all voters!"

A man said, "Publicity, that's right. The principle is perfectly clear in the law, one taxpayer's child is supposed to get the same service as another taxpayer's child. We should write letters to the papers."

Mr. Baer said, "Wait a minute. Letters I don't think mean anything, but I've got a public relations firm; I'll tell them to take a little time off my food specialties and use it for the school. They can use their own know-how, how to do it; they're the experts."

This was moved, seconded and passed, while Murray Logan whispered to Vladek, "He's Marijane Garlic Mayonnaise. He had a twelve-year-old girl in very bad shape that Mrs. Adler helped in her old private class. He bought this building for her, along with a couple of other parents."

Harry Vladek was musing over how it felt to be a parent who could buy a building for a school that would help your child, while the committee reports continued. Some time later, to Harry's dismay, the business turned to financing, and there was a vote to hold a fund-raising theater party for which each couple with a child in the school would have to sell "at least" five pairs of orchestra seats at sixty dollars a pair. Let's get this straightened out now, he thought, and put up his hand.

"My name is Harry Vladek," he said when he was recognized, "and I'm brand new here. In the school and in the county. I work for a big insurance company, and I was lucky enough to get a transfer here so my boy can go to the school. But I just don't know anybody yet that I can sell tickets to for sixty dollars. That's an awful lot of money for my kind of people."

Mrs. Rose said, "It's an awful lot of money for most of us. You can get rid of your tickets, though. We've got to. It doesn't matter if you try a hundred people and ninety-five say no just as long as the others say yes."

He sat down, already calculating. Well, Mr. Crine at the office. He was a bachelor and he did go to the theater. Maybe work up an office raffle for another pair. Or two pairs. Then there was, let's see, the real estate dealer who had sold them the house, the lawyer they'd used for the closing—

Well. It had been explained to him that the tuition, while decidedly not nominal, eighteen hundred dollars a year in fact, did not cover the cost per child. Somebody had to pay for the speech therapist, the dance therapist, the full-time psychologist and the part-time psychiatrist, and all the others, and it might as well be Mr. Crine at the office. And the lawyer.

And half an hour later Mrs. Rose looked at the agenda, checked off an item and said, "That seems to be all for tonight. Mr. and Mrs. Perry brought us some very nice cookies, and we all know that Mrs. Howe's coffee is out of this world. They're in the beginners

room, and we hope you'll all stay to get acquainted.
The meeting is adjourned."

Harry and the Logans joined the polite surge to
the beginners room, where Tommy spent his mornings.
"There's Miss Hackett," said Celia Logan. That was
the beginners' teacher. She saw them and came over,
smiling. Harry had seen her only in a tentlike smock,
her armor against chocolate milk, finger paints and
sudden jets from the "water play" corner of the room.
Without it she was handsomely middle-aged in a
green pants suit.

"I'm glad you parents have met," she said. "I
wanted to tell you that your little boys are getting
along nicely. They're forming a sort of conspiracy
against the others in the class. Vern swipes their toys
and gives them to Tommy."

"He *does?*" cried Logan.

"Yes, indeed. I think he's beginning to relate. And,
Mr. Vladek, Tommy's taken his thumb out of his
mouth for minutes at a time. At least half a dozen
times this morning, without my saying a word."

Harry said excitedly, "You know, I thought I noticed he was tapering off. I couldn't be sure. You're
positive about that?"

"Absolutely," she said. "And I bluffed him into
drawing a face. He gave me that glare of his when the
others were drawing; so I started to take the paper
away. He grabbed it back and scribbled a kind of
Picasso-ish face in one second flat. I wanted to save it
for Mrs. Vladek and you, but Tommy got it and
shredded it in that methodical way he has."

"I wish I could have seen it," said Vladek.

"There'll be others. I can see the prospect of real
improvement in your boys," she said, including the
Logans in her smile. "I have a private case afternoons
that's really tricky. A nine-year-old boy, like Tommy.
He's not bad except for one thing. He thinks Donald
Duck is out to get him. His parents somehow managed
to convince themselves for two years that he was kid-

ding them, in spite of three broken TV picture tubes. Then they went to a psychiatrist and learned the score. Excuse me, I want to talk to Mrs. Adler."

Logan shook his head and said, "I guess we could be worse off, Vladek. Vern giving something to another boy! How do you like that?"

"I like it," his wife said radiantly.

"And did you hear about that other boy? Poor kid. When I hear about something like that— And then there was the Baer girl. I always think it's worse when it's a little girl because, you know, you worry with little girls that somebody will take advantage; but our boys'll make out, Vladek. You heard what Miss Hackett said."

Harry was suddenly impatient to get home to his wife. "I don't think I'll stay for coffee, or do they expect you to?"

"No, no, leave when you like."

"I have a half-hour drive," he said apologetically and went through the golden oak doors, past the ugly but fireproof staircase, out onto the graveled parking lot. His real reason was that he wanted very much to get home before Margaret fell asleep so he could tell her about the thumb-sucking. Things were happening, definite things, after only a month. And Tommy drew a face. And Miss Hackett said—

He stopped in the middle of the lot. He had remembered about Dr. Nicholson, and besides, what was it, exactly, that Miss Hackett had said? Anything about a normal life? Not anything about a cure? "Real improvement," she said, but improvement how far?

He lit a cigarette, turned and plowed his way back through the parents to Mrs. Adler. "Mrs. Adler," he said, "may I see you just for a moment?"

She came with him immediately out of earshot of the others. "Did you enjoy the meeting, Mr. Vladek?"

"Oh, sure. What I wanted to see you about is that I have to make a decision. I don't know what to do. I don't know who to go to. It would help a lot if you could tell me, well, what are Tommy's chances?"

She waited a moment before she responded. "Are you considering committing him, Mr. Vladek?" she demanded.

"No, it's not exactly that. It's—well, what can you tell me, Mrs. Adler? I know a month isn't much. But is he ever going to be like everybody else?"

He could see from her face that she had done this before and had hated it. She said patiently, " 'Everybody else,' Mr. Vladek, includes some terrible people who just don't happen, technically, to be handicapped. Our objective isn't to make Tommy like 'everybody else.' It's just to help him to become the best and most rewarding Tommy Vladek he can."

"Yes, but what's going to happen later on? I mean, if Margaret and I—if anything happens to us?"

She was suffering. "There is simply no way to know, Mr. Vladek," she said gently. "I wouldn't give up hope. But I can't tell you to expect miracles."

Margaret wasn't asleep; she was waiting up for him, in the small living room of the small new house. "How was he?" Vladek asked, as each of them had asked the other on returning home for seven years.

She looked as though she had been crying, but she was calm enough. "Not too bad. I had to lie down with him to get him to go to bed. He took his gland-gunk well, though. He licked the spoon."

"That's good," he said and told her about the drawing of the face, about the conspiracy with little Vern Logan, about the thumb-sucking. He could see how pleased she was, but she only said: "Dr. Nicholson called again."

"I told him not to bother you!"

"He didn't bother me, Harry. He was very nice. I promised him you'd call him back."

"It's eleven o'clock, Margaret. I'll call him in the morning."

"No, I said tonight, no matter what time. He's waiting, and he said to be sure and reverse the charges."

"I wish I'd never answered the son of a bitch's letter," he burst out and then, apologetically: "Is there any coffee? I didn't stay for it at the school."

She had put the water on to boil when she heard the car whine into the driveway, and the instant coffee was already in the cup. She poured it and said, "You have to talk to him, Harry. He has to know tonight."

"Know tonight! Know tonight," he mimicked savagely. He scalded his lips on the coffee cup and said, "What do you want me to do, Margaret? How do I make a decision like this? Today I picked up the phone and called the company psychologist, and when his secretary answered, I said I had the wrong number. I didn't know what to say to him."

"I'm not trying to pressure you, Harry. But he has to know."

Vladek put down the cup and lit his fiftieth cigarette of the day. The little dining room—it wasn't that, it was a half breakfast alcove off the tiny kitchen, but they called it a dining room even to each other—was full of Tommy. The new paint on the wall where Tommy had peeled off the cups-and-spoons wallpaper. The Tommy-proof latch on the stove. The one odd aqua seat that didn't match the others on the kitchen chairs, where Tommy had methodically gouged it with the handle of his spoon. He said, "I know what my mother would tell me, talk to the priest. Maybe I should. But we've never even been to Mass here."

Margaret sat down and helped herself to one of his cigarettes. She was still a good-looking woman. She hadn't gained a pound since Tommy was born, although she usually looked tired. She said, carefully and straightforwardly, "We agreed, Harry. You said you would talk to Mrs. Adler, and you've done that. We said if she didn't think Tommy would ever straighten out we'd talk to Dr. Nicholson. I know it's hard on you, and I know I'm not much help. But I don't know what to do, and I have to let you decide."

Harry looked at his wife, lovingly and hopelessly, and at that moment the phone rang. It was, of course, Dr. Nicholson.

"I haven't made a decision," said Harry Vladek at once. "You're rushing me, Dr. Nicholson."

The distant voice was calm and assured. "No, Mr. Vladek, it's not me that's rushing you. The other boy's heart gave out an hour ago. That's what's rushing you."

"You mean he's dead?" cried Vladek.

"He's on the heart-lung machine, Mr. Vladek. We can hold him for at least eighteen hours, maybe twenty-four. The brain is all right. We're getting very good waves on the oscilloscope. The tissue match with your boy is satisfactory. Better than satisfactory. There's a flight out of JFK at six fifteen in the morning, and I've reserved space for yourself, your wife and Tommy. You'll be met at the airport. You can be here by noon; so we have time. Only just time, Mr. Vladek. It's up to you now."

Vladek said furiously, "I can't decide that! Don't you understand? I don't know how."

"I do understand, Mr. Vladek," said the distant voice and, strangely, Vladek thought, it seemed he did. "I have a suggestion. Would you like to come down anyhow? I think it might help you to see the other boy, and you can talk to his parents. They feel they owe you something even for going this far, and they want to thank you."

"Oh, no!" cried Vladek.

The doctor went on: "All they want is for their boy to have a life. They don't expect anything but that. They'll give you custody of the child—your child, yours and theirs. He's a very fine little boy, Mr. Vladek. Eight years old. Reads beautifully. Makes model airplanes.

They let him ride his bike because he was so sensible and reliable, and the accident wasn't his fault. The truck came right up on the sidewalk and hit him."

Harry was trembling. "That's like giving me a bribe," he said harshly. "That's telling me I can trade Tommy in for somebody smarter and nicer."

"I didn't mean it that way, Mr. Vladek. I only wanted you to know the kind of a boy you can save."

"You don't even know the operation's going to work!"

"No," agreed the doctor. "Not positively. I can tell you that we've transplanted animals, including primates, and human cadavers, and one pair of terminal cases; but you're right, we've never had a transplant into a well body. I've shown you all the records, Mr. Vladek. We went over them with your own doctor when we first talked about this possibility, five months ago. This is the first case since then when the match was close and there was a real hope for success, but you're right, it's still unproved. Unless you help us prove it. For what it's worth, I think it will work. But no one can be sure."

Margaret had left the kitchen, but Vladek knew where she was from the scratchy click in the earpiece: in the bedroom, listening on the extension phone. He said at last, "I can't say now, Dr. Nicholson. I'll call you back in—in half an hour. I can't do any more than that right now."

"That's a great deal, Mr. Vladek. I'll be waiting right here for your call."

Harry sat down and drank the rest of his coffee. You had to be an expert in a lot of things to get along, he was thinking. What did he know about brain transplants? In one way, a lot. He knew that the surgery part was supposed to be straightforward, but the tissue rejection was the problem, but Dr. Nicholson thought he had that licked. He knew that every doctor he had talked to, and he had now talked to seven of them, had agreed that medically it was probably sound enough, and that every one of them had carefully clammed up when he got the conversation around to whether it was right. It was his decision, not theirs, they all said, sometimes just by their silence. But who was he to decide?

Margaret appeared in the doorway. "Harry. Let's go upstairs and look at Tommy."

He said harshly, "Is that supposed to make it easier for me to murder my son?"

She said, "We talked that out, Harry, and we agreed it isn't murder. Whatever it is. I only think that Tommy ought to be with us when we decide, even if he doesn't know what we're deciding."

The two of them stood next to the outsize crib that held their son, looking in the night light at the long fair lashes against the chubby cheeks and the pouted lips around the thumb. Reading. Model airplanes. Riding a bike. Against a quick sketch of a face and the occasional, cherished, tempestuous, bruising flurry of kisses.

Vladek stayed there the full half hour and then, as he had promised, went back to the kitchen, picked up the phone and began to dial.

THE ENGINEER

When writers collaborate, it often happens that one of them takes off in a direction which the other fellow simply can't or won't follow. So sometimes quite long chunks of real, printable copy get thrown away, and tempers fray. This almost never happened when Cyril and I worked together. Our first drafts, of course, needed a lot of revision and polishing, and they got them, but structurally they almost always survived unchanged into print. But there was one exception. In *Gladiator-at-Law* we were intrigued with the idea of a "political engineer" (in the same sense that Eisenhower was a "political general"), but it went nowhere in the novel, and we took it out. A few months later it occurred to us that the scene we had cut was practically a short story in itself, so we put it through the typewriter again and it came out this way.

IT WAS VERY SIMPLE. Some combination of low temperature and high pressure had forced something from the seepage at the ocean bottom into combination with something in the water around them.

And the impregnable armor around Subatlantic Oil's drilling chamber had discovered a weakness.

On the television screen it looked more serious than it was—so Muhlenhoff told himself, staring at it grimly. You get down more than a mile, and you're bound to have little technical problems. That's why deep-sea oil wells were still there.

Still, it did look kind of serious. The water driving in the pitted faults had the pressure of eighteen hundred meters behind it, and where it struck it did not splash—it battered and destroyed. As Muhlenhoff watched, a bulkhead collapsed in an explosion of spray; the remote camera caught a tiny driblet of the scattering brine, and the picture in the screen fluttered and shrank, and came back with a wavering sidewise pulse.

Muhlenhoff flicked off the screen and marched into the room where the Engineering Board was waiting in attitudes of flabby panic.

As he swept his hand through his snow-white crew cut and called the board to order, a dispatch was handed to him—a preliminary report from a quickly-dispatched company trouble-shooter team. He read it to the board, stone-faced.

A veteran heat-transfer man, the first to recover, growled:

"Some vibration thing—and seepage from the oil pool. Sloppy drilling!" He sneered. "Big deal! So a couple hundred meters of shaft have to be plugged and pumped. So six or eight compartments go pop. Since when did we start to believe the cack Research and Development hands out? Armor's armor. Sure it pops —when something makes it pop. If Atlantic oil was easy to get at, it wouldn't be here waiting for us now. Put a gang on the job. Find out what happened, make sure it doesn't happen again. Big deal!"

Muhlenhoff smiled his attractive smile. "Breck," he said, "thank God you've got guts. Perhaps we were in a bit of a panic. Gentlemen, I hope we'll all take heart from Mr. Breck's level-headed—what did you say, Breck?"

Breck didn't look up. He was pawing through the dispatch Muhlenhoff had dropped to the table. *"Nine-*inch plate," he read aloud, white-faced. "And time of installation, not quite seven weeks ago. If this goes on in a straight line—" he grabbed for a pocket slide-rule

—"we have, uh—" he swallowed—"less time than the probable error," he finished.

"Breck!" Muhlenhoff yelled. "Where are you going?"

The veteran heat-transfer man said grimly as he sped through the door: "To find a submarine."

The rest of the Engineering Board was suddenly pulling chairs toward the trouble-shooting team's dispatch. Muhlenhoff slammed a fist on the table.

"Stop it," he said evenly. "The next man who leaves the meeting will have his contract canceled. Is that clear, gentlemen? Good. We will now proceed to get organized."

He had them; they were listening. He said forcefully: "I want a task force consisting of a petrochemist, a vibrations man, a hydrostatics man and a structural engineer. Co-opt mathematicians and computermen as needed. I will have all machines capable of handling Fourier series and up cleared for your use. The work of the task force will be divided into two phases. For Phase One, members will keep their staffs as small as possible. The objective of Phase One is to find the cause of the leaks and predict whether similar leaks are likely elsewhere in the project. On receiving a first approximation from the force I will proceed to set up Phase Two, to deal with countermeasures."

He paused. "Gentlemen," he said, "we must not lose our nerves. We must not panic. Possibly the most serious technical crisis in Atlantic's history lies before us. Your most important job is to maintain—at all times—a cheerful, courageous attitude. We cannot, repeat cannot, afford to have the sub-technical staff of the project panicked for lack of a good example from us." He drilled each of them in turn with a long glare. "And," he finished, "if I hear of anyone suddenly discovering emergency business ashore, the man who does it better get fitted for a sludgemonkey's suit, because that's what he'll be tomorrow. Clear?"

Each of the executives assumed some version of a

cheerful, courageous attitude. They looked ghastly, even to themselves.

Muhlenhoff stalked into his private office, the nerve-center of the whole bulkheaded works.

In Muhlenhoff's private office, you would never know you were 1,800 meters below the surface of the sea. It looked like any oilman's brass-hat office anywhere, complete to the beautiful blonde outside the door (but white-faced and trembling), the potted palm (though the ends of its fronds vibrated gently), and the typical section chief bursting in in the typical flap. "Sir," he whined, frenzied, "Section Six has pinholed! The corrosion—"

"Handle it!" barked Muhlenhoff, and slammed the door. Section Six be damned! What did it matter if a few of the old bulkheads pinholed and filled? The central chambers were safe, until they could lick whatever it was that was corroding. The point was, you had to stay with it and get out the oil; because if you didn't prove your lease, PetroMex would. Mexican oil wanted those reserves mighty badly.

Muhlenhoff knew how to handle an emergency. Back away from it. Get a fresh slant. Above all, *don't panic*.

He slapped a button that guaranteed no interruption and irritably, seeking distraction, picked up his latest copy of the *New New Review*—for he was, among other things, an intellectual as time allowed.

Under the magazine was the latest of several confidential communications from the home office. Muhlenhoff growled and tossed the magazine aside. He re-read what Priestley had had to say:

"I know you understand the importance of beating our Spic friends to the Atlantic deep reserves, so I won't give you a hard time about it. I'll just pass it on the way Lundstrom gave it to me: 'Tell Muhlenhoff he'll come back on the Board or on a board, and no alibis or excuses.' Get it? Well—"

Hell. Muhlenhoff threw the sheet down and tried to think about the damned corrosion-leakage situation.

But he didn't try for long. There was, he realized, no point at all in him thinking about the problem. For one thing, he no longer had the equipment.

Muhlenhoff realized, wonderingly, that he hadn't opened a table of integrals for ten years; he doubted that he could find his way around the pages well enough to run down a tricky form. He had come up pretty fast through the huge technical staff of Atlantic. First he had been a geologist in the procurement section, one of those boots-and-leather-jacket guys who spent his days in rough, tough blasting and drilling and his nights in rarefied scientific air, correlating and integrating the findings of the day. Next he had been a Chief Geologist, chairborne director of youngsters, now and then tackling a muddled report with Theory of Least Squares and Gibbs Phase Rule that magically separated dross from limpid fact . . . or, he admitted wryly, at least turning the muddled reports over to mathematicians who specialized in those disciplines.

Next he had been a Raw Materials Committee member who knew that drilling and figuring weren't the almighty things he had supposed them when he was a kid, who began to see the Big Picture of off-shore leases and depreciation allowances; of power and fusible rocks and steel for the machines, butane for the drills, plastics for the pipelines, metals for the circuits, the computers, the doors, windows, walls, tools, utilities. A committeeman who began to see that a friendly beer poured for the right resources-commission man was really more important than Least Squares or Phase Rule, because a resources commissioner who didn't get along with you might get along, for instance, with somebody from Coastwide, and allot to Coastwide the next available block of leases—thus working grievous harm to Atlantic and the billions it served. A committeeman who began to see that the Big Picture meant

government and science leaning chummily against each
other, government setting science new and challenging
tasks like the billion-barrel procurement program,
science backing government with all its tremendous
prestige. You consume my waste hydrocarbons,
Muhlenhoff thought comfortably, and I'll consume
yours.

Thus mined, smelted and milled, Muhlenhoff was
tempered for higher things. For the first, the technical
directorate of an entire Atlantic Sub-Sea Petroleum
Corporation district, and all wells, fields, pipelines,
stills, storage fields, transport, fabrication and maintenance appertaining thereto. Honors piled upon honors.
And then—

He glanced around him at the comfortable office.
The top. Nothing to be added but voting stock and
Board membership—and those within his grasp, if only
he weathered this last crisis. And then the rarefied
height he occupied alone.

And, by God, he thought, I do a damn good job
of it! Pleasurably he reviewed his conduct at the meeting; he had already forgotten his panic. Those shaking
fools would have brought the roof down on us, he
thought savagely. A few gallons of water in an unim-
portant shaft, and they're set to message the home office, run for the surface, abandon the whole project.
The Big Picture! They didn't see it, and they never
would. He might, he admitted, not be able to chase
an integral form through a table, but by God he could
give the orders to those who would. The thing was organized now; the project was rolling; the task force had
its job mapped out; and somehow, although he would
not do a jot of the brain-wearing, eyestraining, actual
work, it would be *his* job, because he had initiated it.
He thought of the flat, dark square miles of calcareous
ooze outside, under which lay the biggest proved un-
tapped petroleum reserve in the world. Sector Fortyone,
it was called on the hydrographic charts.

Perhaps, some day, the charts would say: *Muhlenhoff Basin*.

Well, why not?

The emergency intercom was flickering its red call light pusillanimously. Muhlenhoff calmly lifted the handset off its cradle and ignored the tinny bleat. When you gave an order, you had to leave the men alone to carry it out.

He relaxed in his chair and picked up a book from the desk. He was, among other things, a student of Old American History, as time permitted.

Fifteen minutes now, he promised himself, with the heroic past. And then back to work refreshed!

Muhlenhoff plunged into the book. He had schooled himself to concentration; he hardly noticed when the pleading noise from the intercom finally gave up trying to attract his attention. The book was a study of that Mexican War in which the United States had been so astonishingly deprived of Texas, Oklahoma and points west under the infamous Peace of Galveston. The story was well told; Muhlenhoff was lost in its story from the first page.

Good thumbnail sketch of Presidente Lopez, artistically contrasted with the United States' Whitmore. More-in-sorrow-than-in-anger off-the-cuff psychoanalysis of the crackpot Texan, Byerly, derisively known to Mexicans as "El Cacafuego." Byerly's raid at the head of his screwball irredentists, their prompt annihilation by the Mexican Third Armored Regiment, Byerly's impeccably legal trial and execution at Tehuantepec. Stiff diplomatic note from the United States. Bland answer: Please mind your business, Señores, and we will mind ours. Stiffer diplomatic note. We said *please,* Señores, and can we not let it go at that? *Very* stiff diplomatic note; and Latin temper flares at last: Mexico severs relations.

Bad to worse. Worse to worst.

Massacre of Mexican nationals at San Antonio. Bland refusal of the United States federal government to interfere in "local police problem" of punishing the guilty. Mexican Third Armored raids San Antone, arrests the murderers (feted for weeks, their faces in the papers, their proud boasts of butchery retold everywhere), and hangs them before recrossing the border.

United States declares war. United States loses war—outmaneuvered, outgeneraled, out-logisticated, outgunned, outmanned.

And outfought.

Said the author:

"The colossal blow this cold military fact delivered to the United States collective ego is inconceivable to us today. Only a study of contemporary comment can make it real to the historian: The choked hysteria of the newspapers, the raging tides of suicides, Whitmore's impeachment and trial, the forced resignations of the entire General Staff—all these serve only to sketch in the national mood.

"Clearly something had happened to the military power which, within less than five decades previous, had annihilated the war machines of the Cominform and the Third Reich.

"We have the words of the contemporary military analyst, Osgood Ferguson, to explain it:

"The rise of the so-called 'political general' means a decline in the efficiency of the army. Other things being equal, an undistracted professional beats an officer who is half soldier and half politician. A general who makes it his sole job to win a war will infallibly defeat an opponent who, by choice or constraint, must offend no voters of enemy ancestry, destroy no cultural or religious shrines highly regarded by the press, show leniency when leniency is fashionable at home, display condign firmness when voters demand it (though it cause his zone of communications to blaze up into a fury of guerrilla clashes), choose his invasion routes to please a state department apprehensive of potential future ententes.

"It is unfortunate that most of Ferguson's documentation was lost when his home was burned during the unsettled years after the war. But we know that what Mexico's Presidente Lopez said to his staff was: 'My generals, win me this war.' And this entire volume does not have enough space to record what the United States generals were told by the White House, the Congress as a whole, the Committees on Military affairs, the Special Committees on Conduct of the War, the State Department, the Commerce Department, the Interior Department, the Director of the Budget, the War Manpower Commission, the Republican National Committee, the Democratic National Committee, the Steel lobby, the Oil lobby, the Labor lobby, the political journals, the daily newspapers, the broadcasters, the ministry, the Granges, the Chambers of Commerce. However, we do know—unhappily—that the United States generals obeyed their orders. This sorry fact was inscribed indelibly on the record at the Peace of Galveston."

Muhlenhoff yawned and closed the book. An amusing theory, he thought, but thin. Political generals? Nonsense.

He was glad to see that his subordinates had given up their attempt to pass responsibility for the immediate problem to his shoulders; the intercom had been silent for many minutes now. It only showed, he thought comfortably, that they had absorbed his leading better than they knew.

He glanced regretfully at the door that had sheltered him, for this precious refreshing interlude, from the shocks of the project outside. Well, the interlude was over; now to see about this leakage thing. Muhlenhoff made a note, in his tidy card-catalog mind, to have

Maintenance on the carpet. The door was bulging out of true. Incredible sloppiness! And some damned fool had shut the locks in the ventilating system. The air was becoming stuffy.

Aggressive and confident, the political engineer pressed the release that opened the door to the greatest shock of all.

NIGHTMARE WITH ZEPPELINS

Elsewhere I have mentioned Cyril's incomplete Civil War novel, *The Crater*. The opening chapters introduced his viewpoint character, an English journalist. I liked the character; I liked the background material; and I used them verbatim in this short story.

THE ZEPPELIN dirigible balloons bombed London again last night and I got little sleep what with the fire brigades clanging down the street and the antiaircraft guns banging away. Bad news in the morning post. A plain card from Emmie to let me know that Sam's gone, fast and without much pain. She didn't say, but I suppose it was the flu, which makes him at least the fifth of the old lib-lab boys taken off this winter. And why not? We're in our seventies and eighties. It's high time.

Shaw said as much the other day when I met him on the steps of the Museum reading room, he striding in, I doddering out. In that brutal, flippant way of his, he was rather funny about how old Harry Lewes was standing in the way of youngsters like himself, but I can't bring myself to put his remarks down; they would be a little too painful to contemplate.

Well, he's quite recovered from that business with his foot that gave us all such a fright. Barring the 'flu, he may live to my age, and about 1939 bright youngsters now unborn will be watching him like hawks for the smallest sign of rigidity, of eccentricity, and saying complacently: "Grand old boy, G.B.S. Such a pity he's going the least bit soft upstairs." And I shall by then be watching from Olympus, and chuckling.

Enough of him. He has the most extraordinary way of getting into everybody's conversation, though it is true that my own conversation does wander, these bad days. I did not think that the second decade of the twentieth century would be like this, though, as I have excellent reason to be, I am glad it is not worse.

I am really quite unhappy and uncomfortable as I sit here at the old desk. Though all the world knows I don't hold with personal service for the young and healthy, I am no longer a member of either of those classes. I do miss the ministrations of Bagley, who at this moment is probably lying in a frozen trench and even more uncomfortable than I. I can't seem to build as warm a fire as he used to. The coals won't go right. Luckily, I know what to do when I am unhappy and uncomfortable: work.

Anyway, Wells is back from France. He has been talking, he says, to some people at the Cavendish Laboratory, wherever that is. He told me we must make a "radium bomb." I wanted to ask: "Must we, Wells? Must we, *really?*"

He says the great virtue of a radium bomb is that it explodes *and keeps on exploding*—for hours, days, weeks. The italics are Wells's—one could hear them in his rather high-pitched voice—and he is welcome to them.

I once saw an explosion which would have interested Wells and, although it did not *keep on exploding,* it was as much of an explosion as I ever care to see.

I thought of telling him so. But, if he believed me, there would be a hue and a cry—I wonder, was I ever once as *consecrated* as he?—and if he did not, he might all the same use it for the subject of one of his "scientific" romances. After I am gone, of course, but surely that event cannot be long delayed, and in any case that would spoil it. And I want the work. I do not think I have another book remaining—forty-one fat volumes will have to do—but this can hardly be a book.

A short essay; it must be short if it is not to become an autobiography and, though I have resisted few temptations in my life, I mean to fight that one off to the end. That was another jeer of Shaw's. Well, he scored off me, for I confess that some such thought had stirred in my mind.

My lifelong struggle with voice and pen against social injustice had barely begun in 1864, and yet I had played a part in three major work stoppages, published perhaps a dozen pamphlets and was the editor and principal contributor of the still-remembered *Labour's Voice*. I write with what must look like immodesty only to explain how it was that I came to the attention of Miss Carlotta Cox. I was working with the furious energy of a very young man who has discovered his vocation, and no doubt Miss Cox mistook my daemon—now long gone, alas!—for me.

Miss Cox was a member of that considerable group of ruling-class Englishmen and women who devote time, thought and money to improving the lot of the workingman. Everybody knows of good Josiah Wedgewood, Mr. William Morris, Miss Nightingale; they were the great ones. Perhaps I alone today remember Miss Cox, but there were hundreds like her and pray God there will always be.

She was then a spinster in her sixties and had spent most of her life giving away her fortune. She had gone once in her youth to the cotton mills whence that fortune had come, and knew after her first horrified look what her course must be. She instructed her man of business to sell all her shares in that Inferno of sweated labour and for the next forty years, as she always put it, attempted to make restitution.

She summoned me, in short, to her then-celebrated

stationer's shop and, between waiting on purchasers of nibs and foolscap, told me her plan. I was to go to Africa.

Across the Atlantic, America was at war within herself. The rebellious South was holding on, not with any hope of subduing the North, but in the expectation of support from England.

England herself was divided. Though England had abolished slavery on her own soil almost a century earlier, still the detestable practise had its apologists, and there were those who held the rude blacks incapable of assuming the dignities of freedom. I was to seek out the Dahomeys and the Congolese on their own grounds and give the lie to those who thought them less than men.

"Tell England," said Miss Cox, "that the so-called primitive Negroes possessed great empires when our fathers lived in wattle huts. Tell England that the black lawgivers of Solomon's time are true representatives of their people, and that the monstrous caricature of the plantation black is a venal creation of an ignoble class!"

She spoke like that, but she also handed me a cheque for two hundred and fifty pounds to defray my expenses of travel and to subsidize a wide distribution of the numbers of *Labour's Voice* which would contain my correspondence.

Despite her sometimes grotesque manner, Miss Cox's project was not an unwise one. Whatever enlightenment could be bought at a price of two hundred and fifty pounds was a blow at human slavery. Nor, being barely twenty, was I much distressed by the thought of a voyage to strange lands.

In no time at all, I had turned the direction of *Labour's Voice* over to my tested friends and contributors Mr. Samuel Blackett and Miss Emma Chatto (they married a month later) and in a week I was aboard a French "composite ship," iron of frame and wooden of skin, bound for a port on the Dark Continent, the home of mystery and enchantment.

So we thought of it in those days and so, in almost as great degree, do we think of it today, though I venture to suppose that, once this great war is over, those same creations of Count Zeppelin which bombed me last night may dispel some of the mystery, exorcise the enchantment and bring light into the darkness. May it be so, though I trust that whatever discoveries these aeronauts of tomorrow may bring will not repeat the discovery Herr Faesch made known to me in 1864.

The squalor of ocean travel in those days is no part of my story. It existed and I endured it for what seemed like an eternity, but at last I bade farewell to *Le Flamant* and all her roaches, rats and stench. Nor does it become this memoir to discuss the tragic failure of the mission Miss Cox had given me.

(Those few who remember my *Peoples of the Earth* will perhaps also remember the account given in the chapter I entitled "Africa Journeyings." Those, still fewer, whose perception revealed to them an unaccountable gap between the putrid sore throat with which I was afflicted at the headwaters of the Congo and my leave taking on the Gold Coast will find herewith the chronicle of the missing days).

It is enough to say that I found no empires in 1864. If they had existed, and I believe they had, they were vanished with Sheba's Queen. I did, however, find Herr Faesch. Or he found me.

How shall I describe Herr Faesch for you? I shan't, Shaw notwithstanding, permit myself so hackneyed a term as "hardy Swiss"; I am not so far removed from the youthful spring of creation as that. Yet Swiss he was, and surely hardy as well, for he discovered me (or his natives did) a thousand miles from a community of Europeans, deserted by my own bearers, nearer to death than ever I have been since. He told me that I tried thrice to kill him, in my delirium; but he nursed me well and I lived. As you see.

He was a scientific man, a student of Nature's ways, and a healer, though one cure was beyond him. For, sick though I was, he was more ravaged by destructive illness than I. I woke in a firelit hut with a rank poultice at my throat and a naked savage daubing at my brow, and I was terrified; no, not of the native, but of the awful cadaverous face, ghost-white, that frowned down at me from the shadows.

That was my first sight of Herr Faesch.

When, a day later, I came able to sit up and to talk, I found him a gentle and brave man, whose English was every bit as good as my own, whose knowledge surpassed that of any human I met before or since. But the mark of death was on him. In that equatorial jungle, his complexion was alabaster. Ruling the reckless black warriors who served him, his strength yet was less than a child's. In those steaming afternoons when I hardly dared stir from my cot for fear of stroke, he wore gloves and a woollen scarf at his neck.

We had, in all, three days together. As I regained my health, his health dwindled.

He introduced himself to me as a native of Geneva, that colorful city on the finest lake of the Alps. He listened courteously while I told him of my own errand and did me, and the absent Miss Cox, the courtesy of admiring the spirit which prompted it—though he was not sanguine of my prospects of finding the empires.

He said nothing of what had brought him to this remote wilderness, but I thought I knew. Surely gold. Perhaps diamonds or some other gem, but I thought not; gold was much more plausible.

I had picked up enough of the native dialect to catch perhaps one word in twenty of what he said to his natives and they to him—enough, at any rate, to know that when he left me in their charge for some hours, that first day, he was going to a hole in the ground. It could only be a mine, and what, I asked myself, would a European trouble to mine in the heart of unexplored Africa but gold?

I was wrong, of course. It was not gold at all.

Wells says that they are doing astonishing things at the Cavendish Laboratory, but I do think that Herr Faesch might have astonished even Wells. Certainly he astonished me. On the second day of my convalescence, I found myself strong enough to be up and walking about.

Say that I was prying. Perhaps I was. It was oppressively hot—I dared not venture outside—and yet I was too restless to lie abed waiting for Herr Faesch's return. I found myself examining the objects on his camp table and there were, indeed, nuggets. But the nuggets were not gold. They were a silvery metal, blackened and discolored, but surely without gold's yellow hue; they were rather small, like irregular lark's eggs, and yet they were queerly heavy. Perhaps there was a score of them, aggregatng about a pound or two.

I rattled them thoughtfully in my hand, and then observed that across the tent, in a laboratory jar with a glass stopper, there were perhaps a dozen more—yes, and in yet another place in that tent, in a pottery dish, another clutch of the things. I thought to bring them close together so that I might compare them. I fetched the jar and set it on the table; I went after the pellets in the pottery dish.

Herr Faesch's voice, shaking with emotion, halted me. "Mr. Lewes!" he whispered harshly. "Stop, sir!"

I turned, and there was the man, his eyes wide with horror, standing at the flap of the tent. I made my apologies, but he waved them aside.

"No, no," he croaked, "I know you meant no harm. But I tell you, Mr. Lewes, you were very near to death a moment ago."

I glanced at the pellets. "From these, Herr Faesch?"

"Yes, Mr. Lewes. From those." He tottered into the tent and retrieved the pottery dish from my hands. Back to its corner it went; then the jar, back across the tent again. "They must not come together. No, sir," he said, nodding thoughtfully, though I had said nothing with which he might have been agreeing, "they must not come together."

He sat down. "Mr. Lewes," he whispered, "have you ever heard of uranium?" I had not. "Or of pitchblende? No? Well," he said earnestly, "I assure you that you will. These ingots, Mr. Lewes, are uranium, but not the standard metal of commerce. No, sir. They are a rare variant form, indistinguishable by the most delicate of chemical tests from the ordinary metal, but possessed of characteristics which are—I shall merely say 'wonderful,' Mr. Lewes, for I dare not use the term which comes first to mind."

"Remarkable," said I, feeling that some such response was wanted.

He agreed. "Remarkable indeed, my dear Mr. Lewes! You really cannot imagine how remarkable. Suppose I should tell you that the mere act of placing those few nuggets you discovered in close juxtaposition to each other would liberate an immense amount of energy. Suppose I should tell you that if a certain critical quantity of this metal should be joined together, an explosion would result. Eh, Mr. Lewes? What of that?"

I could only say again, "Remarkable, Herr Faesch." I knew nothing else to say. I was not yet one-and-twenty, I had had no interest in making chemists' stinks, and much of what he said was Greek to me— or was science to me, which was worse, for I should have understood the Greek tolerably well. Also a certain apprehension lingered in my mind. That terrible white face, those fired eyes, his agitated speech—I could not be blamed, I think. I believed he might be mad. And though I listened, I heard not, as he went on to tell me of what his discovery might mean.

The next morning he thrust a sheaf of manuscript at me. "Read, Mr. Lewes!" he commanded me and went off to his mine; but something went wrong. I drowsed through a few pages and made nothing of them except that he thought in some way his nuggets had affected his health. There was a radiant glow in the mine, and the natives believed that glow meant sickness and in time death, and Herr Faesch had come to agree with the natives. A pity, I thought absently, turning in for a nap.

A monstrous smashing sound awakened me. No one was about. I ran out, thrusting aside the tent flap and there, over a hill, through the interstices of the trees, I saw a huge and angry cloud. I don't know how to describe it; I have never since seen its like, and pray God the world never shall again until the end of time.

Five miles away it must have been, but there was heat from it; the tent itself was charred. Tall it was—I don't know how tall, stretching straight and thin from the ground to a toadstool crown shot with lightnings.

The natives came after a time, and though they were desperately afraid, I managed to get from them that it was Herr Faesch's mine that had blown up, along with Herr Faesch and a dozen of themselves. More than that, they would not say.

And I never saw one of them again. In a few days, when I was strong enough, I made my way back to the river and there I was found and helped—I have never known by whom. Half dazed, my fever recurring, I remember only endless journeying, until I found myself near a port.

Yes, there was explosion enough for any man.

That whippersnapper Wells! Suppose, I put it to you, that some such "radium bomb" should be made. Conceive the captains of Kaiser Will's dirigible fleet possessed of a few nuggets apiece such as those Herr Faesch owned half a century ago. Imagine them cruising above the city of London, sowing their dragon's-teeth pellets in certain predetermined places, until in time a sufficient accumulation was reached to set the whole thing off. Can you think what horror it might set free upon the world?

And so I have never told this story, nor ever would if it were not for those same Zeppelin dirigible balloons. Even now I think it best to withhold it until this war is over, a year or two perhaps. (And that will probably make it posthumous—if only to accommodate Shaw—but no matter.)

I have seen a great deal. I know what I know, and I feel what I feel; and I tell you, this marvelous decade that stretches ahead of us after this present war will open new windows on freedom for the human race. Can it be doubted? Poor Bagley's letters from the trenches tell me that the very *poilus* and Tommies are determined to build a new world on the ruins of the old.

Well, perhaps Herr Faesch's nuggets will help them, these wiser, nobler children of the dawn who are to follow us. They will know what to make of them. One thing is sure: Count Zeppelin has made it impossible for Herr Faesch's metal ever to be used for war. Fighting on the ground itself was terrible enough; this new dimension of warfare will end it. Imagine sending dirigibles across the skies to sow such horrors! Imagine what monstrous brains might plan such an assault! Merciful heaven. They wouldn't dare.

CRITICAL MASS

After Cyril's death, his widow turned up a bale of paper and delivered it to me: incomplete manuscripts, notes, one or two projects that he had completed and, for one reason or another, not published. Most of the fragments I ultimately completed, over a period of fifteen years, and they appear in this volume. "Critical Mass" wasn't exactly one of them, it was *three* of them —four, if you count some notes of my own, made for a story of that title I started and abandoned in 1954.

THE NEUTRON was a plump young man named Walter Chase, though what he thought he was was a brand-new Engineering graduate, sitting mummified and content with the other 3,876 in Eastern's class of '98, waiting for his sheepskin.

The university glee club sang the ancient scholastic song *Gaudeamus Igitur* with mournful respect and creamy phrasing, for they and most of the graduates, faculty members, parents, relatives and friends present in the field house thought it was a hymn instead of the rowdy drinking song it was. It was a warm June day, conducive to reverence. Of Eastern's 3,877 graduating men and women only three had majored in classical languages. What those three would do for a living from July on was problematical. But in June they had at least the pleasure of an internal chuckle over the many bowed heads.

Walter Chase's was bowed with the rest. He was

of the Civil Engineering breed, and he had learned more about concrete in the four years just ended than you would think possible. Something called The Cement Research and Development Institute, whose vague but inspirational commercials were regularly on the TV screens, had located Walter as a promising high-school graduate. He was then considering the glamorous and expensive field of nuclear physics. A plausible C.R.D.I. field man had signed him up and set him straight. It took twelve years to make a nuclear physicist. Now, wasn't that a hell of a long time to wait for the good things of life? Now, here was something he ought to consider: Four years. In four years he could walk right into a job with automatic pay raises, protected seniority, stock participation *and* Blue Everything, paid by the company. Concrete was the big industry of tomorrow. The C.R.D.I. was deeply concerned over the lack of interest in concrete engineering, and it was prepared to do something about it: Full four-year scholarship, tuition, living costs and pocket money. Well?

Walter signed. He was a level-headed eighteen-year-old. He had been living with a pinch-penny aunt and uncle, his parents dead; the chance of the aunt and uncle financing twelve years of nuclear studies for him he estimated to lie midway between the incredible and the impossible.

Two solid hours dwindled past in addresses by the Chancellor, the Governor of the State and a couple of other politicos receiving honorary degrees. Walter Chase allowed the words to slip past him as though they were dreams, although many of them concerned his own specialty: shelters. You knew what politician talk was. He and the 3,876 others were coldly realistic enough to know that C.S.B. was a long way from being enacted into law, much less concrete-and-steel Civilian Shelters in fact. Otherwise why would the Institute have to keep begging for students to give scholarships to? He drowsed. Then, as if with an absent-minded start, the program ended.

Everybody flocked away onto the campus.

In the hubbub was all the talk of the time: "Nice weather, but, Kee-*rist!* those speeches!" "Who d'ya like in the All-Star?" "Nothing wrong with C.S.B. if it's *handled* right, but you take and throw a couple thousand warheads over the Pole and—" "My feet hurt." Chase heard without listening. He was in a hurry.

There was no one he wanted to meet, no special friend or family. The aunt and uncle were not present at his graduation. When it had become clear from their letters that they expected him to pay back what they had spent to care for him as soon as he began earning money, he telephoned them. Collect. He suggested that they sue him for the money or, alternatively, take a flying jump for themselves. It effectively closed out a relationship he loathed.

Chase saw, approaching him across the crowded campus, another relationship it was time to close out. The relationship's name was Douglasina MacArthur Baggett, a brand-new graduate in journalism. She was pretty and she had in tow two older persons who Chase perceived to be her parents. "Walter," she bubbled, "I don't believe you were even *looking* for me! Meet Daddy and Mom."

Walter Chase allowed his hand to be shaken. Baggett *père* was something in Health, Education and Welfare that had awakened Walter's interest at one time; but as Douglasina had let it slip that Daddy had been passed over for promotion three years running, Walter's interest had run out. The old fool now began babbling about how young fellows like Walter would, through the Civilian Shelters Bill, really give the country the top-dog Summit bargaining position that would pull old Zhdetchnikov's cork for him. The mother simpered: "So *you're* the young man! We've heard so much about you in Douglasina's letters. I tell you, why don't you come and spend the All-Star weekend with us in Chevy Chase?"

Walter asked blankly: "Why?"

"Why?" said Mrs. Baggett in a faint voice, after a perceptible pause. Walter smiled warmly.

"After all," he said, shrugging, "boy-girl college friendships. . . . She's a fine girl, Mrs. Baggett. Delighted to have met you, Mr. Baggett. Doug, maybe we'll run into each other again, eh?" He clapped her on the shoulder and slipped away.

Once screened from the sight of their faces, he sighed. In some ways he would miss her, he thought. Well. On to the future!

In the dormitory he snapped the locks on his luggage, already packed, carried them down to be stowed in the luggage compartment of the airport bus and then circulated gently through the halls. He had in four years at Eastern made eleven Good Contacts and thirty-six Possibles, and he had an hour or two before his plane to joke with, shake the hand of, or congratulate the nine of those on the list who shared his dorm. He fooled the fools and flattered the flatterable, but in his wake a few of his classmates grimly said: "That young son of a bitch is going to go far, unless he runs out of faces to step on."

Having attended to his nine he charitably spread some of his remaining time among the couple dozen Outside Chances he ran into. To a sincere, but confused, servo-mech specialist he said, man-to-man, "Well, Frankie, what's the big decision? Made up your mind about the job yet?"

The servo-mech man clutched him and told him his tale of woe. "God no, Walt. I don't know *which* way to turn. Missile R and D's offering me a commission right away, captain inside of two years. But who wants to be a soldier all his life? And there's nothing in private industry for inertial guidance, you know.

Damn it, Walt, if only they let you resign from the service after a couple years!" Chase said something more or less comforting and moved on. He was careful not to chuckle until he was out of sight.

Poor Frankie! Got himself educated in what amounted to a military speciality—who else could afford servo-mechanisms?—and discovered he hated the Army.

Still, Chase meditated while nodding, smiling and handshaking, thirty years as an Engineering Officer might not be so bad. As it was one of the alternatives open to himself—that was what C.S.B. was all about —he allowed his mind to drift over the prospects. It wasn't like the bad old days of fighting. A flat and rigid policy of atomic retaliation had been U. S. military doctrine for fifty-three years, and backing it up was a large, well-trained U. S. military establishment of career men. And the regulations said *career*. The only way out short of thirty-year retirement was with a can tied to your tail and a taint to your name. He dismissed that thirty-year dead end with light contempt, as he had before.

The air-raid warning sirens began to howl their undulating hysteria.

Chase sighed and glanced at his watch. Not too bad. He should still be able to make his plane. Everyone around him was saying things like, "Ah, damn it!" or "Oh, dear," or *"Jeez!"* But they were all dutifully following the arrows and the "S" signs that dotted the campus.

Chase trailed along. He was kind of annoyed, but nothing could really spoil his day. The first shelter he came to was full up. The freshman raid warden stood at the door—Chase had been a raid warden himself three years before—chanting: "Basement filled to capacity, folks. Please proceed to Chemistry building. Don't block the exit, folks. Basement here filled—"

Because of the extra crowd caused by the graduation the Chemistry building basement was filled, too,

but Chase got into the Administration building and
sat down to wait. Like everybody else. Women fussed
about their dresses—they always had, in every air raid
drill he had taken part in, say, four a week for fifty-two
weeks of each year for the nearly twenty years since
he had been old enough to toddle alongside his late
mother and father. Men grumbled about missing appointments. *They* always had. But for the most part
the battery-fed air-raid lights gleamed equably on
them all, the warden fussed with the air conditioner
and the younger folk smooched in the corners.

It wasn't a bad shelter, Walter Chase thought.
The Law School basement was a mess—too high a pH
in the mortar mix, and the aggregate showing hygro-
scopic tendencies because of some clown not watching
his rock crusher, so the walls were cracked and damp.
Chemistry's had been poured in a freeze. Well, naturally it began to sinter and flake. This was better; trust
the Chancellor to make sure his own nest was downy!
Of course, in a *raid* none of them would be worth a
hoot; but there weren't to be any real raids. Ever.

A jet plane's ripping path sounded overhead.

Evidently this was going to be a full-dress affair,
at least regional in scope. They didn't throw simulated
manned-bomber attacks for a purely local do. Walter
frowned. It had suddenly occurred to him that with the
air-transport flight lanes screwed up by military fighters on simulated missions everything within a thousand
miles might be rerouted into stack patterns. What the
devil would that do to his plane's departure time?

Then he smiled forebearingly. He was, in a way,
pleased to be annoyed. It meant he was entering into
the adult world of appointments and passages. They
said that when a raid drill began to be a damn interruption instead of a welcome break from classes and a
chance to smooch, then, brother, you were growing up.
He guessed he was growing up.

"Goddam foolishness," growled the man who sat
next to Chase on the bench, as though it were a per-

sonal attack. More jets shredded sound overhead and he glared at Chase. Walter inventoried his English shoes, seal ring and pale cigar and at once engaged him in conversation. The man was some graduate's father; they had got separated in the raid drill, and Pop was sore as a tramped bunion. The whole drill thing was damned childishness, didn't Walter see that? And *vindictive* damned childishness when they chose to throw one on graduation day of a major university. If only Crockhouse had been elected in '96 instead of Braden, with his packed ballots in Indiana and Puerto Rico!

Here Walter Chase's interest cooled, because Pop sounded like a politician, revealed himself to be a Nationalist and thus was out of power. But there was no escaping the bench. What Pop objected bitterly to was the multiple levels of expense. Here the drill was knocking men out of production, but the damn Middle-Road Congress said they had to be paid anyhow. And if the Defense Department was making it a full-scale simulated raid, did Walter know what that meant? That meant that there went thirty or forty *Nineveh Ables* at a hundred and fifty thousand dollars apiece, and was that enough? No. Then they sent up four or five *Tyres* at ninety thousand apiece to knock down the *Ninevehs*. Did that make sense? He paused to glare at Walter Chase.

Walter said, "Well, that's the Cold War for you. Say, who d'you like in the All-Star—" He didn't get to finish the sentence.

"L.A." snapped Pop, without losing a beat. "Get the damn monkey-business over with, that's what I say. I'm a sneak-puncher and I'm proud of it. If we'd put our man in the White House instead of that psalmsinging Braden there wouldn't *be* any Moscow or Peking or Calcutta by now and we wouldn't be sitting here on our butts!"

Somebody clawed through from the bench in front;

with horror, Chase recognized old man Baggett. But Douglasina's Daddy did not recognize him. Flushed with rage and politics he had eyes only for the sneak-punch advocate. "You're right it's monkey-business, fat-mouth!" he snarled. "No thanks to you and your Crock-house we aren't dead in this cellar instead of safe and secure! President Braden is a hundred percent pledged to the C.S.B., God bless it, and—"

The rest of his sentence and Sneak-Punch's angry reply were drowned out by a further flight of jets overhead, and then the *wham-wham-wham* of inter-ceptor missiles blowing simulated attackers out of the sky.

Somehow, heaven knew how, Walter Chase man-aged to sneak away, inching through the packed rows of benches. As soon as the All Clear siren toots began he was up and out, ignoring the freshman warden's puppy-like yaps that they should remain in their seats until the front benches had been emptied—

Routine. It was all strictly routine.

Out on the campus, Chase headed for the airport in earnest, and was delighted to find that his flight was still on time. How lucky he was, he thought, with more pride than gratitude. "What are you, sir?" asked the robot baggage-checker, and he said, "Washington," with pleasure. He was on his way. He was headed for Washington, where Dr. Hines of The Cement Re-search and Development Institute would assign him to his job, doubtless the first rung of a dizzying climb to wealth and fame. He was a young man on his way. Or so he thought. He did not know that he was only a neutron ambling toward events.

ii

Arturo Denzer, in the same sense, was a nucleus. He knew no more about it than Walter Chase.

Denzer woke to the rays of a rising sun and the snarl of his wake-up clock. He took a vitamin capsule,

an aspirin tablet, a thyroid injection; a mildly euphoric
jolt of racemic amphetamine sulphate; caffeine via
three cups of black coffee with sucaryl; and nicotine
via a chain of nonfiltering filter-tip cigarettes. He
then left his apartment for the offices of *Nature's Way
Magazine,* which he edited.

June's blossom was in the air, and so was the tin-
gle of the All-Star Game Number One. The elevator
operator said to him respectfully, "Who d'ya like in
the All-Star game, Mr. Denzer?" Denzer turned the
operator's conversation circuit off with a handwave.
He didn't feel like talking to a robot at least until the
aspirin began to work.

Absent-mindedly he waved a cab to him and
climbed in. Only after it took off did he notice, to his
dismay, that he had picked a Black-and-White fleet
hack. They were salty and picturesque—and couldn't
be turned off. The damned thing would probably call
him "Mac."

"Who ya like inna All-Star, Mac?" the cab asked
genially, and Denzer winched. Trapped, he drummed
his fingers on the armrest and stared at the Jefferson
Memorial in its sea of amusement rides and hot-dog
stands. "Who ya like inna All-Star, Mac?" it asked
again, genially and relentlessly. It would go on asking
until he answered.

"Yanks," Denzer grunted. Next time he'd watch
what he was doing and get a sleek, black Rippington
Livery with a respectful BBC accent.

"Them bums?" groaned the cab derisively.
"Watcha think Craffany's up to?"

Craffany was the Yankee manager. Denzer knew
that he had benched three of his star players over the
last weekend—indeed, it was impossible to avoid
knowing it. Denzer struck out wildly: "Saving them
for the All-Star, I guess."

The cab grunted and said: "Maybe. My guess,
Fliederwick's in a slump so Craffany benched him
and pulled Hockins and Waller so it'd look like he

was saving 'em for the All-Star. Ya notice Fliederwick
was 0 for 11 in the first game with Navy?"

Denzer gritted his teeth and slumped down in the
seat. After a moment the cab grunted and said: "Maybe. My guess is Fliederwick's in a slump so Craffany
benched him and pulled. . . ." It went through it twice
more before Denzer and his hangover could stand no
more.

"I hate baseball," he said distinctly.

The cab said at once, "Well, it's a free country.
Say, ya see Braden's speech on the C.S.B. last night?"

"I did."

"He really gave it to them, right? You got to
watch those traitors. Course, like Crockhouse says,
where we going to get the money?"

"Print it, I imagine," snarled Denzer.

"Figgers don't lie. We already got a gross national
debt of $87,912.02 per person, you know that? Tack
on the cost of the Civilian Shelters and whaddya got?"

Denzer's headache was becoming cataclysmic. He
rubbed his temples feverishly.

"Figgers don't lie. We already got a gross national . . ."

Desperate situations require desperate measures.
"I hate p-politics too," he said, stuttering a little. Normally he didn't like smutty talk.

The cab broke off and growled: "Watch ya language, Mac. This is a respectable fleet."

The cab corkscrewed down to a landing in North
Arlington-Alex and said, "Here y'are, Mac." Denzer
paid it and stepped from the windy terrace of the
Press House onto a crowded westbound corridor. He
hoped in a way that the cab wouldn't turn him in to a
gossip columnist. In another way he didn't care.

Around him buzzed the noise of the All-Star and
the C.S.B. ". . . Craffany . . . $87,912.02, and at *least*
$6,175.50 for Shelters . . . Foxy Framish and Little Joe

Fliederwick . . . well, this *is* next year . . . nah, you sneak-punch 'em a couple thousand missiles over the Pole and . . . needs a year in the minors."

"Hello, Denzer," someone said. It was Maggie Frome, his assistant.

"Hello, Maggie," he said, and added automatically: "Who do you like in the All-Star game?"

In a low, ferocious voice she muttered: "You can take the All-Star game, tie it up in a b-b-b-brassiere and dump it in a Civilian Shelter. I am sick of the subject. *Both* subjects."

He flushed at her language and protested: "Really, Maggie!"

"Sorry," she grunted, sounding as though she didn't mean it. He contrasted her surly intransigence with his own reasoned remarks to the cab and tolerantly shook his head. Of course, he could have been taken the wrong way . . . He began to worry.

They stepped off together at the *Nature's Way* offices. Sales & Promotion was paralyzed. Instead of rows of talkers at rows of desks, phoning prospects out of city directories and high-pressuring them into subscriptions, the department was curdled into little knots of people cheerfully squabbling about the C.S.B. and the All-Stars. Denzer sighed and led the girl on into Transmission. The gang should have been tuning up the works, ready to shoot the next issue into seven million home facsimile receivers. Instead, the gang was talking All-Stars and C.S.B. It was the same in Typography, the same in Layout, the same in Editorial.

The door closed behind them, isolating their twin office from the babble. Blessed silence. "Maggie," he said, "I have a headache. Will you please work on the final paste-ups and cutting for me? There isn't anything that should give you any trouble."

"Okay, Denzer," she said, and retreated to her half of the office with the magazine dummy. Denzer felt a momentary pang of conscience. The issue was way overset and cutting it was a stinker of a job to pass on to Maggie Frome. Still, that was what you had assistants for, wasn't it?

He studied her, covertly, as she bent over the dummy. She was a nice-looking girl, even if she was a hangover from the administration of President Danton and his Century of the Common Woman. Maggie's mother had been something of an integrationist leader in Sandusky, Ohio, and had flocked to Washington as one mote in Danton's crackpot horde, bringing her subteenage daughter Maggie. No doubt there had been a father, but Maggie never mentioned him. The mother had died in a car crash that looked like suicide after Danton lost all fifty-four states in his bid for re-election, but by then Maggie was a pert teenager who moved in with cousins in Arlington-Alex and she stayed on. Must just like Washington, Denzer thought. Not because of Female Integration, though. Danton's Century of the Common Woman had lasted just four years.

He winced a little as he remembered her coarseness of speech. She was round and brown-haired. You couldn't have everything.

Denzer leaned back and shut his eyes. The hubbub outside the office was just barely audible for a moment—some red-hot argument over the Gottshalk Committee's Shelter Report or Fliederwick's R.B.I. had swelled briefly to the shrieking stage—and then died away again. Heretically he wondered what the point was in getting excited over baseball or the building or nonbuilding of air-raid shelters capable of housing every American all the time. One was as remote from reality as the other.

"Sorry, Denzer."

He sat up, banging his knee on his desk.

"Lousy staff work, I'm afraid. Here's the Aztec Cocawine piece and no lab verification on the test results." She was waving red-crayoned galleys in his face.

He looked at the scrawling red question-mark over the neat columns of type with distaste. *Nature's Way* promised its seven million subscribers that it would not sell them anything that would kill them; or, at least, that if it did kill them nobody would be able to hang it on the product directly. At substantial expense, they maintained a facility to prove this point. It was called The Nature's Way National Impartial Research Foundation. "So call the lab," he said.

"No good, Denzer. Front-office memo last month. Lab verifications must be *in* writing *with* notary's seal *on* hand before the issue goes to bed."

"Cripes," he protested, "that means somebody's got to go clear over to Lobby House." He did not meet her eye. Going over to Lobby House was a worthwhile break in the day's routine; the free snack-bar and free bar-bar the lobbies maintained was up to the best expense-account standards, and everyone enjoyed talking to the kooks in the lab. They were so odd.

"I'll go if you want, Denzer," she said, startling him into looking at her.

"But the issue—"

"Did most of it last night, Denzer. The Aztec story is all that's left."

"We'll both go," he said, rising. She had earned it; he needed a bromo and a shot of B-1 vitagunk in the Lobby House snack-bar; and since there would be two of them in the cab he had a ruse for cutting out the cab's talk about All-Stars and the C.S.B.

The ruse was this: As soon as the cab took off he flung his arms around her and bore her back against the arm rest.

The cab chuckled and winked at them with its rear-view lens, as it was programmed to do. They discussed proofreading, the vacation sked and the choice of lead commercials for the next issue of *Nature's Way*

in soft whispers into each other's ears all the way to
Lobby House, while the cab winked and chuckled at
them every fifteen seconds.

The knocks on the 93rd floor were under the care
of a sort of half-breed race of semi-kooks. These were
science majors who had minored in journalism . . . or in
marrying rich . . . and thus wandered into press agentry
for scientific concerns. As liaison men between *Nature's Way* and the test-tube manipulators the semi-
kooks occupied an uncertain middle ground. It sometimes made them belligerent. Denzer and the girl were
let in to see the Director of Bennington's Division, a
Dr. Bennington, and Denzer said: "We came for the
Aztec Cocawine certification."

Dr. Bennington boomed: "Damn right! Coming
right up! Say, who's gonna take it in the Game?" He
thumped a button on his desk and in a moment a tall,
stooped youth with a proudly beaked nose swept in
and threw a document on his desk. "Thanks, Valendora. Lessee here, um, yeah. Says it's harmless to the
nerves, ya-ta-ta, ya-ta-ta, all signed and stamped.
Anything else today, Arturo? Gland extract, fake a
heroin prescription, shot of Scotch?"

The beaked youth said loftily: "Our findings are
set forth precisely, Dr. Bennington. The fluid contains
an alkaloid which appreciably eroded the myelin
sheaths of the autonomic nerve trunks."

Denzer blanched, but the semi-kook administra-
tor agreed carelessly, "Right, that's what I said. It's
that word 'appreciably.' Anything less than 'markedly,'
we write it down as negative." He slipped it in an
envelope that was already marked *Confidential Findings, Aztec Wine of Coca Corporation, Sponsor,* and
sailed it across to Denzer. "Well, what about C.S.B.,
boy? They gonna get us dug in before it's too late?"
He made them promise to stop in at the snack-bar or
bar-bar before leaving the building, then offered them
a drink out of his private stock. They refused, of

course. That was just his way of saying good-bye. It was the only way he knew to end a conversation.

With the certification in his pocket and the issue locked up, Denzer began to feel as though he might live, especially if he made it to the B-1 vitagunk dispenser in the snack-bar. He took Maggie Frome by the arm and was astonished to feel her shaking.

"Sorry, Denzer. I'm not crying, really. If somebody's going to sell crazy-making dope to the public, why *shouldn't* it be you and me? We're no better than anybody else, d-d-damn it!"

He said uncomfortably, "Maybe a drink's not such a bad idea. What do you say?"

"I'd love it," she sobbed. But then the sirens began to wail and they said, "Damn it," and "Oh, dear" —respectively, she did and he did—and they took their bearings by the signs and made for the shelters. Under Lobby House was nothing like enough space, so the air-raid shelter was the interior parts of the 10th through 85th floors, away from the flying glass of the curtain walls but not too near the elevator shafts. It was not a bad shelter, actually. It was proof against any bomb that the world had ever known, up to say, early 1943.

There was plenty of room but not enough benches. Maggie and Denzer found a place on the floor where they could put their backs against a wall, and he allowed her to lean against his shoulder. She wasn't such a bad kid, he thought sympathetically, especially as the perfume in her hair was pleasant in his nostrils. There wasn't anything really *wrong* with Female Integration. Maggie wasn't a *nut*. Take baseball. Why, that was the Integrationist's major conquest, when women demanded and got equal representation on every major-league team in spite of the fact that they could not throw or run on competitive terms with men. They said that if all the teams had the same number of women it wouldn't matter. And it hadn't. And Integrationists were still crowing over the victory; and yet Maggie had refused to fall into the All-Star hysteria.

A roar like an outboard motor in the crown of your hat shook the building; A. A. "carpet" cannon laying a sheet of sudden death for missiles across the sky above them. Denzer relaxed. His headache was almost gone. He inclined his head to rest his cheek against Maggie's hair. Even with a hangover, it had been pleasant in the cab with his arms around her. He had been kind of looking forward to the return trip. If Denzer were indeed a nucleus, as in a way he was, he was beginning to feel a certain tugging of binding energy toward certain other nuclear particles.

As soon as the noise stopped, he thought he would speak to her.

The noise stopped. The voices of the men beside them bellowed into the sudden quiet: "—damned foolish idea of Therapeutic War was exploded ten years ago! And that's what we'd be if your idiot Crockhouse was in—exploded!"

And the man next to him: "At least Crockhouse wouldn't have us sitting in these fool imitation shelters! He'd *do* something."

"Whadya think *Braden* wants, for God's sake? Not these things. He's right on the record for C.S.B."

And then Maggie Frome, breathing fire, her head no longer resting on Denzer's shoulder: "What the hell is so great about C.S.B.? Shelters, no shelters, can't you get it through your head that if this keeps up we're *dead*? Dear God above, deliver me from fools, baseball players and p-p-politicians!"

Denzer tried to look as though he'd never met her; he was white-faced. Round, yes, sweet-smelling, yes, warm—but how could he ever get used to her dirty *talk*?

iii

If Denzer was a nucleus and Walter Chase a neutron, what can we call the President of the United States? He played a part. Without him nothing could happen. Perhaps what he did was to shape the life of the neutron before fission happened; in that sense one could call him a "moderator." This was an apt term for President Braden.

On this bright June morning in Washington—not Arlington-Alex or the bedroom municipalities in Maryland but the little old Federal District itself—the President of the United States held what was still called a "press" conference. He was late. The cathode-tube "newspapermen" grumbled a little as Secret Service men frisked them, but it was habit. They were used to being frisked, ever since that fanatic Alaskan nationalist publisher emptied a .32 at then-President Hutzmeyer in '83. And they were used to now-President Braden being late.

They rose when President Braden came in. As usual, he protested in his pleasant adopted border-South accent: "Please, ladies, please, gentlemen, don't bother—" So they sat down and smiled, and waited while Braden arranged some papers on his desk. He always did that. He never referred to them during the session, because he didn't have to, but every week there was the minute or two of silence in the room while the President, his rimless glasses gleaming studiously, pursed his lips over the documents in their red, blue and cream-colored folders.

He looked up and beamed.

Unobtrusive camera-eyes mounted flush with the walls of the conference room began to record. The elephantine Giuseppe von Bortoski, N.B.C. Washington bureau chief, incomparably senior correspondent, was privileged to lead off. He did: "Good morning, Mr. President. Do you have a statement for us today?"

"Nothing prepared, Joseph. It's been a quiet week, hasn't it?"

Von Bortoski said solemnly, "Not for Craffany," and everybody roared. Von Bortoski waited out his laugh and said: "But seriously, Mr. President, is there any comment on the radar picket situation?"

The President paused, then looked faintly surprised. "I didn't know there was a 'situation,' Joseph. Our radar picket vessels off the Atlantic and Pacific coasts have been pulled in approximately two hundred miles. They all have the new microradar; they don't have to be so far out. This gives us a gratifying economy, since the closer we can pull them in the fewer ships we need to stick out there on picket duty. Is that what you wanted to know, Joseph?"

"No, Mr. President. I was referring to Representative Simpson's telecast yesterday. He alleged that the new radars haven't been adequately field-tested. Said the move was premature and, well, dangerous."

The President paused, then looked faintly angry. "I seem to recall that Illinois Simpson. A Democrat." Everybody nodded. "I am surprised that you are taking up our time, Joseph, with the wild charges that emanate with monotonous regularity from the Party of Treason." Everyone looked at the stout N.B.C. man with annoyance. The President turned toward a young lady correspondent, paused, and said, "Miss Bannerman, do you have a question?"

She did. What about the Civilian Shelters Bill?

The President paused, grinned and said, "I'm for it." He got a small laugh.

"I mean, Mr. President, what is its status now? As the leader of your Party, is it going to go through?"

The President paused longer than usual. Everyone in the room knew what he was waiting for, though it was a convention of the Press Conference to pretend he was answering off the cuff. At last the other end

of the transprompter circuit got its signals cleared and
the President said levelly: "As the leader of my
Party, Miss Bannerman, I can say this thing is being
hammered out. Slower than some of us would wish,
true. But it will be done. It is the platform of my
Party; on that platform I was elected in '98; and I
have not the reputation of going back on my pledges."
He inclined his head to an approving stir among the
correspondents.

Von Bortoski made a mental calculation. He decided that the press conference had supplied enough
matter for his upcoming newscast and to hell with the
rest of them. "Thank you, Mr. President," he said.
The other reporters swore under their breaths once
more at the tyranny of the senior-correspondent rule,
the President rose smiling and the armed guards
stepped away from the doors.

C.S.B., C.S.B., the President mediated. Someday
he would have to ask a question himself and find out
just what this C.S.B. was all about. No doubt the R
& I desk that fed him answers or speeches via the
transprompter could tell him. He promised himself he
would get around to it first thing, say, Monday. Or
wait, wasn't Monday the first All-Star game?

A swift conveyor belt whisked him from the An-
nex to the Old White House and an escalator to the
Oval Room. His personal secretary ventured to say:
"You made good time, Governor. There's thirty-five
minutes clear before the first appointment. How about
a nap?"

President Braden snapped: "I see General Standish has been talking to you again, Murray. Tell that
quack when I want doctoring I'll ask for it, and get me
a drink."

The President, who liked to think he was a hard-
riding, hard-drinking southern gentleman, although he
had been a New Jersey accountant until he was thirty,

sipped a glass of mineral water lightly tinted with whiskey, decided he was refreshed and buzzed for the first appointment to start ahead of time.

The first appointment was with Senator Horton of Indiana. While he was coming in, the transprompter whispered into the President's ear: "Call him David, not Dave. No wife. Ex-professor, for God's sake. Watch him."

The President rose, smiling, and gripped Horton's hand with warmth and the pressure of an old campaigner. "It's a great pleasure, David. How's Indiana shaping up for next year? Lose all your best seniors?"

Senator Horton had a shock of gray hair, a mournful face and a surprisingly springy, lean body for a fifty-year-old ex-professor. He said abruptly: "I don't follow the school's football schedule. Mr. President, I want something."

"Unto the half of my kingdom," Braden said gaily, attempting to throw him off balance.

Horton gave him a meager smile. "I want you to bear down on the Civilian Shelters Bill. You are, after all, committed to it. It helped elect you. But twenty-two months have gone by and the bill is still in the Public Works Committee. I am on that committee, Mr. President, and it is my impression that I am the only member interested in seeing it enacted into law."

The President said gravely, "That's a mighty serious charge, David. One I cannot act on without the fullest—"

"Excuse me for interrupting, Mr. President, but your time is valuable and there are some things you needn't bother explaining to me." Deeply affronted, the President stared at him. "Believe me when I say that I've come to you as a last resort. I get only bland evasions from Harkness. The Interior Department—"

Harkness was the committee chairman and he had been Braden's personal campaign manager in the '96 run. The President rose and said, "Excuse *me,* Senator, but I don't permit people to speak about Jim Harkness like that in my presence."

Senator Horton distractedly ran his hands through his shock of hair. "I didn't mean to offend you. God knows I don't mean to offend anyone. Not even the Secretary of Interior, though if he thinks— No, I won't say that. All I want is to get the C.S.B. on the floor and get the construction work under way. Mr. President, how long can all this go on?"

The President remained standing, looked at his watch and said coolly, "All what, David?"

"We are in the fifty-third year of the Political War, Mr. President. Somehow, by a succession of last-minute, hairs-breadth accidents, we have escaped nuclear bombing. It can't go on forever! If the missiles came over the Pole today they'd annihilate this nation, and I don't give one juicy damn that China and Russia would be annihilated in the next forty minutes—"

He was trembling. The President's earphone whispered tinnily: "Hospitalized one year; nervous breakdown. The guard-ports have him covered with sleep guns, sir." That was a relief; but what about this Horton? He was Doane's personal choice, chairman of the National Committee; had Doane put a raving maniac in the Senate? The President remembered, from those young, county-committeeman days when he remembered things clearly, that something like that had happened before. It had been during the Party of Treason's first years—a lunatic from the Northwest got elected to Congress and was mighty embarrassing until he committed suicide. The President, then a schoolboy, had chuckled with the rest of the nation over Congressman Zioncheck; but now he was not chuckling. It was *his* Administration and in the *Senate*. And a member of, God help him, *his* party.

The President did not look toward the guard-ports and the riflemen behind them. He said quietly, "David, I want you to calm down. No pledges have been forgotten and no pledges are going to be violated. I'll speak to Jim Harkness about the Shelter Bill today. That's a promise."

"Thank you," Horton said gratefully, and tried to smile. "I'll hold you to that, sir. Good day."

The President buzzed, not for his next appointment but to talk to his secretary. "Murray, get me Senator Harkness on the phone." And to his chest microphone: "Trans-prompter desk? Get out of circuit. I'll buzz you." He heard the faint carrier tone in his ear die and the guard-ports' click. For the first time since he stepped out of his shower that morning, the President was able to say a word that no one but himself could hear. He said it. It had only one syllable, but it improved his mood very much.

Harkness's voice was resonant and comforting. The President, sometimes nagged by a secret feeling that he was not very bright, knew damned well that he was brighter than Harkness.

He said: "Jim, I've got to wondering about this C.S.B. that you've got in Public Works. The day's young yet and I've had two questions about it. I know we campaigned on it—what is it, exactly?"

Harkness said comfortingly: "It's under control, Brad. That fellow Horton is trying to unbottle it, but we can keep him quiet. He doesn't know the ropes."

"Know that, Jim. I just had him in here, wailing and mad. What's it all about?"

"Why," said Senator Harkness, with something less of assurance in his voice, "it's about building shelters, Brad. Against nuclear attack." He pronounced it "nookyoular," in the approved White House fashion.

"Not quite my point, Jim. I mean—" the President searched for what it was he did mean—"I mean, I can find out the facts and so on, but what's got people so stirred up? Put it this way, Jim: What's your philosophy about the Civilian Shelters Bill?"

"Philosophy?" Harkness sounded vaguely scared.

"Well, I would not know about philosophy, Brad. It's an issue, C.S.B. is, and we're very fortunate to have got it away from the Nationalists. C.S.B.'s very popular." The President sighed inaudibly and relaxed; Senator Harkness was clearly about to launch into one of his famous explanations of things that never needed to be explained. "You see, Brad, an issue is lifeblood to a party. Look over the field today. What's to argue about? Damn little. Everybody knows the Party of Treason is the Party of Treason. Everybody knows the Commies are crazy hoodlums, can't trust 'em. Everybody knows atomic retaliation is the only sound military policy. There, at one sweep, you knock domestic, foreign and military policy off the board and haven't anything left to play with except C.S.B." He paused for breath, but before the President could try to get him back on the track of the question he was rushing on: "It's a godsend, Brad! The Nationalists guessed wrong. They turned C.S.B. down in the name of economy. My opinion, they listened too much to the Defense Department people; naturally the generals didn't want to admit they can't intercept whatever the Commies throw at us, and naturally they want the money for interception instead of shelters. Well, that's all right, too, but the people say the last word. We Middle-Roaders guessed right. We slapped C.S.B. in our platform, and we won. What else is there to say about it? Now, we're not going to turn loose of an issue like that. Fools if we did. The strategy's to milk it along, get it on the floor just before we adjourn for campaign trips and if a Nationalist filibuster kills it, so much the better. That saves it for us for next year! You know, you never get credit in this game for what you've done. Only for what you're going to do. And, *hell,* Brad," he crowed, suddenly exultant as a child who has found a dime in the street, "this thing is good for years! There has to be a big conference committee with the House on financing C.S.B., we haven't even set up liaison with Military Affairs. We've got four more years easy. How's that sound, Brad, eh? Ride right in to reelection in Twenty Oh Oh, the first President of the twenty-first century!"

"Thanks, Jim," said the President, "I knew I could get a straight answer out of you." It was the only way to stop him. Otherwise he might go clear on to the C.S.B. and its effect on the Integrationists, the C.S.B. and Labor, the C.S.B. and Colorado water diversion or the C.S.B. as viewed in the light of Craffany's benching of Little Joe Fliederwick.

And yet, pondered the President, he still didn't know even the question, much less the answer. *Why* was C.S.B. a good issue? The missiles hadn't hit in the past fifty-three years, why should a voting population march to the booths and elect its leaders because of their Shelter philosophy now?

Braden changed the subject. "What do you think of Horton, Jim?"

He could always count on Harkness being frank, at least. "Don't like him. A boat-rocker. You want my advice, Brad? You haven't asked for it, but it's get rid of him. Get the National Committee to put a little money in his district before the primaries."

"I see," said the President, thanked his former campaign manager and hung up.

He took a moment before buzzing Murray for the next appointment to sip his lightly tinted soda water and close his eyes. Well, he'd wasted most of the thirty-five minutes he'd gained, and not even a nap to show for it. Maybe General Standish was right.

Once when Braden was younger, before he was governor of New Jersey, before he was state senator, when he still lived in the old Rumford house on the beach and commuted to Jersey City every day—once he had been a member of the National Guard, what he considered his obligation as a resigned West Pointer. And they had killed two of their obligatory four-hours-a-month one month watching a documentary film on nuclear attack. The arrows marched over the Pole and the picture dissolved to a flight of missiles. The warheads exploded high in air. Then the film went to stock shots, beautifully selected and paced: the experimental houses searing and burning on Yucca Flats, the etched shadows of killed men on the walls of Hiroshima, a forest fire, a desert, empty, and the wind lifting sand-devils. The narration had told how such-and-such kind of construction would be burned within so many miles of Ground Zero. It remarked that forest fires would blaze on every mountain and mentioned matter-of-factly that they wouldn't go out until the winter snow or spring rains, and of course then the ground would be bare and the topsoil would creep as mud down to the oceans. It estimated that then, the year was no later than 1960, a full-scale attack would cost the world 90 percent of its capacity to support life for at least a couple of centuries. Braden had never forgotten that movie.

He had never forgotten it, but he admitted that sometimes he had allowed it to slip out of his mind for a while. This latest while seemed to have lasted quite a few years. Only C.S.B. had brought it back in his recollection.

Because that was the question, the President thought, sipping his tinted soda water. What was the use of C.S.B.? What was the use of any kind of shelters, be they deep as damn-all, if all you had to come out of them to was a burned-out Sahara?

iv

Now that the simulated raid was over everybody was resuming their interrupted errands at once. Denzer was crammed in any-which-way with Maggie Frome wedged under an arm and that kook from the Institute—Venezuela?—gabbling in his ear about computer studies and myelin sheaths.

The elevator jollied them all along. "Don't forget

tomorrow, folks. Be a lot of grandmother's buried tomorrow, eh?" It could not wink, but it giggled and, well, nudged them. Or at least it shook them. It was overloaded with the crowds from the shelter floors, and its compensators flagged, dropping it an inch below the sill of the lobby door, then lifting it. "Sorry, folks," it apologized. "Good night, all!"

Denzer grabbed Maggie's arm. The laboratory man called after him, but he only nodded and tugged the girl away through the crowds, which were mumbling to each other: "Foxy Framish . . . slip 'em a couple thousand nookyoular . . . caught off first . . . *oh, hell.*" The "oh, hells" became general as they reached the main lobby outside of the elevator bays.

Civilian Air Wardens formed chains across the exits. Like fish weirs they chuted the exiting civilians into lines and passed each line through a checkpoint.

"Denzer," groaned Maggie, "I'm cooked. I *never* wear my dosimeter badge with this old green dress."

The wardens were checking every person for his compulsory air-raid equipment. Denzer swore handily, then brightened. They did have their press cards; this *was* official business. Aztec Wine of Coca was a powerful name in industry, and didn't they have a right to take care of its affairs even if they overlooked a few formalities that nobody really took very seriously anyway? He said confidently: "Bet I get us out of it, Maggie. Watch this." And he led her forcefully to the nearest warden. "You, there. Important morale business; here's my card. I'm Denzer of *Nature's Way.* This's my assistant, Frome. I—"

Briskly the warden nodded. "Yes, *sir,* Mr. Denzer. Just come this way." He led them through the purse-seine of wardens, out of the building, into—why, Denzer saw, outraged, into a *police cab.*

"You fixed us fine, Denzer," gloomed Maggie at his side as they got in. He didn't have the spirit to listen to her.

The roundup had bagged nearly fifty hardened criminals, like Denzer and Maggie, caught flagrantly naked of dosimeters and next-of-kin tags. They were a surly lot. Even the C.S.B. adherents among them belligerently protested their treatment; the sneak-punchers were incandescent about the whole thing. Office girls, executives, errand boys, even one hangdog A.R.P. guard himself; they were a motley assortment. The research man, Valendora, was among them, and so was the girl from the Institute's reception room. Valendora saw Denzer and slipped through the crowd toward him, holding a manila envelope as though it contained diphtheria vaccine and he was the first man to arrive at the scene of an epidemic. "Mr. Denzer," he said darkly, "I ask you to assist me. Eleven months of my time and twenty-two computer hours! And this is the only copy. *Statist. Analysis Trans.* expects this by tomorrow at the latest, and—"

Denzer hardly heard. *Statist. Analysis Trans.* was not the only periodical expecting something from one of the fish in this net. With an inner ear Denzer was listening to what his Front Office would say. He was, he saw clearly, about to miss a deadline. Seven million paid-up subscribers would be complaining to the Front Office when their copies were late, and Denzer knew all too well who Front Office would complain to about *that*. He whimpered faintly and reached for an amphetamine tablet, but an A.R.P. cop caught his arm. "Watch it, Mac," said the cop, not unkindly. "No getting rid of evidence there. You got to turn all that stuff in."

Denzer had never been arrested before. He was in a semi-daze while they were waiting to be booked. Ahead of him in line a minor squabble arose—Valendora seemed to be clashing with a plump young fellow in a collegiate crew-cut—but Denzer was paying little attention as he numbly emptied his pockets and put all his possessions on the desk to be locked away for him.

It was not until Maggie Frome repeated his name
for the fifth time that he realized she was talking to
him. She indicated a lanky, homely woman talking
into an autonoter, seemingly on terms of amiable mutual contempt with the police.

"Denzer," Maggie hissed urgently, "that girl over
there. The reporter. Name's Sue-Mary Gribb, and I
know her. Used to work with her on the *Herald*."

"That's nice. Say, Maggie," he moaned, "what
the devil are we going to do about the Aztec Wine of
Coca piece? The Front Office'll have our heads."

"What I'm trying to tell you, Denzer! Give her the
lab report. She'll take it in for us!"

The sun rose in pink glory for Arturo Denzer.

Half blinded by the radiance of sudden, unexpected hope, he staggered back to the desk. Valendora
and the plump youth were still at it, but he pushed
past them, picked up the Nature's Way National Impartial Research Foundation envelope and clawed his
way back to Maggie. "Pencil!" he snapped. She produced one and Denzer scribbled a note to Joe, in Production:

Joe, we're in a jam. Fix this up for us somehow.
Run it pp 34-35, push it through soonest, I've already
got all okays so just jam it in. God bless you. If Front
Office asks where I am I'm dead.

He thought of adding, "Will explain later," but he
wasn't so very sure he could. He thought of kissing
Sue-Mary Gribb; but she was another Female Integrationist, wearing slacks, carrying a corncob pipe; he
only shook her hand briskly and watched her leave.

It was not until she was out the door that he realized why she had been there in the first place.

She was a reporter, gathering names. It was cus-
tomary to run a list of A.R.P. violators in the newspapers. It was inevitable that someone who worked
for *Nature's Way* would see his and Maggie's names

on that list; and it was beyond hope that that someone would fail to show it to the Front Office.

With the help of Sue-Mary Gribb he might have made his deadline, but his troubles were not over. Front Office was solid C.S.B.

"Maggie," he said faintly, "when you left the *Herald,* did you part friends? I mean, do you think they might give us a job?"

The next thing was that they had to wait for their hearing and, in the way of police courts, that took some time. Meanwhile they were all jammed together, noisy and fretful.

The bull-pen roared: "Quiet down, you mokes! You think this is a debating society?" Denzer sighed and changed position slightly so as not to disturb Maggie Frome, again placidly dozing on his shoulder. (This could become a habit, he thought.)

Well, that was something else the Century of the Common Woman had accomplished. They had integrated the lockups, for better or for worse. Not that Maggie, asleep, was deriving the benefit she might from the integrated, but still very loud, yammering of the inmates of the bullpen.

They weren't all A.R.P. violators. A sizeable knot in one corner were clearly common drunks, bellowing about the All-Star Game when they were not singing raucously. They were the chief targets of the bullpen's repeated thunderings for quiet, as its volumetric ears registered an excessive noise level. They must wear out those tapes in a week, Denzer thought.

A diffident finger touched his arm. "Mr. Denzer?" It was the research fellow from the Institute.

Softly, to refrain from disturbing Maggie, he said: "Hello, Venezuela. Make yourself comfortable."

"Valendora, Mr. Denzer."

"Sorry," said Denzer absently, inhaling Maggie's hair.

"I ask you, Mr. Denzer," Valendora said, choos-

ing his words with as much care as though he were
taping a question for his computers, "is it proper that
I should be arrested for being twenty-six feet away
from where I would not be arrested?"

Denzer stared at him. "Come again?" Maggie
stirred restlessly on his shoulder.

"I was two floors below the Foundation, Mr. Denzer, no more," said the research man. "We are not
required to wear dosimeters in the Institute itself. Two
floors is twenty-six feet."

Denzer sighed. This was not a time when he had
patience for nuts. The girl on his shoulder stirred and
he said, "Good morning, Maggie." Valendora swept
on:

"Naturally, Mr. Denzer, it did not occur to me to
go back for my dosimeter. My probably error was
more than twenty-four hours minus, though zero plus,
and it might have been the real attack. I was carrying
a most important document and I could not endanger
it."

Maggie looked at him with faint curiosity and
then twisted around to look at Denzer's face. "The
deadline, Denzer?" she muttered. He crossed his fingers and shrugged.

"Mr. Denzer," cried Valendora, "you are a man
of influence. *Statist. Analysis Trans.* is waiting for this
study—and besides," he added wonderingly, "I suppose if the attack is to come tomorrow someone should
do something about it. Can you not secure justice for
me in this matter?"

Rocked by the sudden vision of himself as a man
of influence, Denzer hardly heard the rest of what the
research man was saying. Maggie Frome pushed herself away from him and stared thoughtfully at Valendora.

"We're all in the same boat, friend," she said
kindly.

Valendora scowled at the floor.

"But what's this about an attack?"

With bitter sarcasm Valendora said, "Nothing at all, Miss Frome. Merely what I have spent eleven months of my time on. *And* twenty-two computer hours."

"I'm impressed, friend. You said something about an attack?"

Valendora said, "You would not understand single-event prediction, Miss Frome. It is a statistical assessment of probabilities. Oh, nothing in itself that has not previously been studied, true; but it is in the establishing of quantitative values for subjective data that I have, I do know, made a contribution." He shrugged moodily. "And by tomorrow? The event, you see. If I have not published before the event it is only a mathematical statement. The test of a theory is the predictions that can be made from it; I have made my prediction. During the All-Star Game, you see—"

"There you are!" cried a new voice.

It was the plump youth who had been quarreling with Valendora at the booking desk. He was still angry. "Baseball," he snapped, "that's all I hear. Can't I make anyone understand that I am a special investigator on Senator Horton's *personal* staff? The senator is waiting to interview me right now! And this man has stolen my thesis!" He put a hand out and briskly pumped Denzer's. "Walter Chase, sir. M.A., C.E., and all the rest of that nonsense," he twinkled, for he had made a quick estimate of Denzer's well-cut clothes and hangdog look and pigeonholed him at once as *second-string executive, subject to flattery.*

"Denzer. *Nature's Way,*" he mumbled, trying to let go of the hand, but Chase hung on.

"I'm in cement, Mr. Denzer," he said. "Did a bit of research—my dissertation, actually—just received another degree—and Senator Horton is most taken by it. Most taken, Mr. Denzer. Unfortunately I've just the one copy, as it happens and it's, well, rather important that it not be lost. It concerns cement, as it affects

our shelter program—and, after all, what *is* a shelter
but cement? Eh? Probably should've been classified
at the start, but—" He shrugged with the faint amused
distaste of the man of science for the bureaucrat. "Anyway, I must have it; the senator must see it with his
own eyes before he'll give me the j— before making
final arrangements. And this man has stolen it."

"Stolen!" screamed Valendora. "Man! It is your
fault, man! I was only—"

"Be careful!" commanded Chase furiously. "Don't
blame *me!* I was merely—"

Denzer felt a tug on his arm. Maggie Frome
winked and led him away, near the group of singing
drunks. They sat down again. "Quieter here!" she
shouted in his ear. "Put your shoulder back, Denzer!
I want to go back to sleep!"

"All right!" he yelled, and helped her settle her
head against him; but in a moment she raised it again.

"Denzer!" she asked over the singing of the group,
"did you hear what your friend from the Institute was
saying? Something about an attack? I had the funny
idea he meant missile attack—a real one, I mean."

"No," he shouted back, "it was only baseball!
All-Star Game, you know."

And he hardly heard the raucous bellowing of
the drunks for the next half hour, inhaling the fragrance of her hair.

They were released at last, Denzer making bail;
the bail corresponded to the amount of their fines for
A.R.P. violation, and small print at the bottom of
their summons pointed out that they could forfeit it
if they chose, thus paying their fines, simply by failing
to appear at the magistrate's trial. They got out just in
time to get the bulldog edition of *Nature's Way* from
a sidewalk scriber.

They looked at once on the spread, pages 34
and 35, expecting anything, even blank pages.

Tragically, the pages were not blank at all.

Pages 34 and 35 had nothing to do with Aztec Wine of Coca. It was a straight news story, headlined:

U. S. MISSILE VULNERABILITY TOTAL IN
ALL-STAR GAME, SAYS GOVERNMENT
STATISTICS EXPERT

From there it got worse. Maggie screamed faintly over Denzer's shoulder as she read parts of it aloud: " 'The obsessive preoccupation of the American public with baseball stems from a bread-and-circuses analogy with ancient Rome. Now, as then, it may lead to our destruction.' Denzer! Does this maniac want us to get lynched?"

"Read on," moaned Denzer, already several laps ahead of her. Neatly boxed on the second page was a digested, sexed-up version of something Denzer recognized faintly as the study of cement in the shelter program Chase had mentioned. What the *Nature's Way* semantic-digester had made of it was:

SHELTERS DEATH TRAPS

Study of the approved construction codes of all American shelter projects indicates that they will not withstand even large chemical explosives.

"I think," sobbed Arturo Denzer, "that I'll cut my throat."

"Not here, Mac," snapped the news-scribing machine. "Move on, will you? *Hey!* Late! Whaddya read?"

Shaking, the couple moved on. "Denzer," Maggie gasped, "where do you think Joe got this stuff?"

"Why, from us, Maggie," Denzer tried to swallow, but his throat was dry. "Didn't you hear Chase before? That was the mix-up at the desk; we must have got his papers, and I suppose what's his-name's, Venezuela's, and bundled them off to Joe. Nice job of rush typography, though," he added absently, staring into space. "Say, Maggie. What Venezuela was talking about. You think there's any truth to it?"

"To what, Denzer?"

"What it says here. Optimum time for the Other Side to strike—during the All-Star Game, it says. You think—?"

Maggie shook her head. "I don't think, Denzer," she said, and they walked on for a moment.

They heard their names called, turned, and were overtaken rapidly by Valendora and the cement engineer. "You!" cried Chase. "You have my thesis!"

"And you have my study!" cried Valendora.

"Not I but humanity," said Denzer sadly, holding out the damp faxed edition of *Nature's Way*.

Valendora, after one white-faced oath in Spanish, took it calmly. He glanced up at the sky for a second, then shrugged. "Someone will not like this. I should estimate," he said thoughtfully, "that within five minutes we will all be back in the *calabozo*."

But he was wrong.

It was actually less than three.

v

It was the third inning, and Craffany had just benched Little Joe Fliederwick. In spite of the sudden ban on air travel the stadium was full. Every television screen in the country followed Little Joe's trudging walk to the dugout.

In the White House, President Braden, shoes off, sipping a can of beer, ignored the insistent buzzing in his ear as long as he could. He wanted to watch the game. "—and the crowd is *roaring*," roared the announcer, "just a-*boiling*, folks! What's Craffany up to? What will he do next? Man, don't we have one going here *today*? Folks, was that the all-important turning point in today's all-im—in today's record-breaking All-Star Game, folks? Well, we'll see. In sixty seconds we'll return to the field, but meanwhile—"

The President allowed his attention to slip away from the commercial and took another pull at his beer. Baseball, now. That was something he could get his teeth into. He'd been a fan since the age of five. All his life. Even during the Century of the Common Woman, when that madman Danton had listened to the Female Lobby and put girls on every second base in the nation. But it had never been this good. This Fliederwick, now, he was *good*.

Diverted, he glanced at the screen. The camera was on Little Joe again, standing at the steps to the dugout, looking up. So were his teammates; and the announcer was saying: "Looks like some more of those air-to-air missile-busters, folks. A huge flight of them. *Way* up. Well, it's good to know our country's defense is being looked after and, say, speaking of defense, what do you suppose Craffany's going to do now that—"

The buzzing returned. The President sighed and spoke to his invisible microphones. "What? Oh. Well, damn it . . . all right."

With a resentful heart he put down the beer can and snapped off the television set. He debated putting his shoes back on. He decided against it, and pulled his chair close to the desk to hide his socks.

The door opened and Senator Horton came in.

"Mr. President," cried Horton, "I want to thank you. There's no doubt your prompt action has saved your country, sir. I imagine you've been filled in on the, ah, incident."

Well, he had been, the President thought, but by Senator Harkness, and maybe the time had come when Jim Harkness' view of world affairs needed a little broadening. "Suppose you tell me about it," he said.

Horton looked faintly perplexed, but said promptly: "It was basically an accident. Two men, working independently, came up with reports, strictly unofficial, but important. One was a graduate student's thesis on shelter construction; happens the boy was looking for

a job, the Cement Research and Development Institute
recommended him to me, he was on his way to see me
when the thing happened. That's how I became involved in it. The other fellow's a lab worker, at least
as far as earning a living's concerned, but he's a mathe-
matician something-or-other and was working out a
problem with his lab's computers. The problem: If the
Reds are going to sneak-punch us, when will they do
it? The answer: today. While we're all off base, with
the All-Star Game. In the old days they'd maybe pick
a presidential election to put one over, just like Hitler
used to pick the long weekends. Now all they need is
a couple of hours when everybody's looking the other
way, you see. All-Star Game's a natural."

The President said mildly, "I can see that without
using a computer, Senator."

"Certainly, sir. But this boy proved it. Like to
meet him, by the way? I've got the lot of them, right
outside."

In for a penny, in for a pound, thought the President, motioning them in. There were three men and a
girl, rather young, rather excited. Senator Horton rattled off introductions. The President gathered the other
two had been involved in the security leak that had
occurred on the reports.

"But I've talked to them," cried Senator Horton,
"and I can't believe there's a grain of malice in all of
them. And what they say, Mr. President, requires immediate action."

"I was under the impression I'd taken immediate
action," said the President. "You asked me to ground
all civilian air traffic so the missile-watchers could have
a clear field; I did. You asked me to put all our defense aircraft airborne; I did. You asked for a
Condition Red defense posture and you got it, all but
the official announcement."

"Yes, Mr. President. The immediate danger may
have been averted, yes. But what about the future?"

"I see," said the President, and paused for a second. Oddly, there was no voice from the prompter in his ear to suggest his next words. He frowned.

"I see," he said again, louder. The tiny voice in his ear said at last:

"Well, sir, uh—" It cleared its throat. "Sir, there seems to be some confusion here. Perhaps you could ask the Senator to continue to brief you."

"Well—" said the President.

"David," whispered the prompter.

"—David, let's get our thinking organized. Why don't you continue to fill me in?"

"Gladly, sir! As you know, I'm Shelters all the way. Always have been. But what this young man here says has shaken me to the core. Mr. Venezuela says—" Valendora grinned sullenly at the rug—"that at this very moment we would be in atoms if it hadn't been for his timely publication of the statistical breakdown of our vulnerability. He's even a little sore about it, Mr. President."

"Sore?"

The senator grinned. "We spoiled his prediction," he explained. "Of course, we saved our own lives . . . The Other Side has computers too; they must have assessed our national preoccupation with baseball. Beyond doubt they intended to strike. Only the commotion his article caused—not only in our own country but, through their embassies, on the Other Side—plus of course your immediate reaction when I telephoned you asking for a Red Alert, kept the missiles from coming down today, sir. I'm certain of it. And this other young fellow, Mr. Chase—" Walter Chase bowed his head modestly—"brought out a lot of data in his term paper, or whatever it was. Seemed like nonsense, sir, so we checked it. Everything he said is not only fact but old stuff; it's been published hundreds of times. Not a word of new material in it." Chase glared. "That's why we've never built deep shelters. They simply won't stand up against massive attack—

and cannot be made to stand up. It's too late for shelters. In building them we're falling into the oldest
strategic trap of human warfare: We're fighting yesterday's war today."

President Braden experienced a sinking feeling
when the earprompter said only, and doubtfully, "Ask
him to go on, sir."

"Go on, si—Go on, David."

"Why," said the senator, astonished, "that's all
there is, Mr. President. The rest is up to you."

President Braden remembered vaguely, as a
youth, stories about the administration of President
—who was it? Truman, or somebody around then.
They said Truman had a sign on his desk that read:
The buck stops here.

His own desk, the President noticed for the first
time, was mirror-smooth. It held no such sign. Apart
from the framed picture of his late wife there was
nothing.

Yet the principle still held, remorselessly, no matter how long he had been able to postpone its applica-
tion. He was the last man in the chain. There was no
one to whom the President could pass the buck. If
it was time for the nation to pick itself up, turn itself
around and head off in a new direction, he was the
only one who could order it to march.

He thought about the alternatives. Say these fellows were right. Say the shelters couldn't keep the nation going in the event of all-out attack. Say the
present alert, so incredibly costly in money and men,
could not be maintained around the clock for any
length of time, which it surely could not. Say the
sneak-punchers were right . . .

But no, thought the President somberly, that avenue had been explored and the end was disaster. You
could never get *all* the opposing missile bases, not
while some were under the sea and some were touring
the highways of the Siberian tundra on trucks and some

were orbital and some were airborne. And it only took a handful of survivors to kill you.

So what was left?

Here and now, everybody was waiting for him to speak—even the little voice in his ear.

The President pushed his chair back and put his feet up on the desk. "You know," he said, wiggling his toes in their Argyle socks, "I once went to school too. True," he said, not apologizing, "it was West Point. That's a good school too, you know. I remember writing a term paper in one of the sociology courses . . . or was it history? No matter. I still recall what I said in that paper. I said wasn't it astonishing that things always got worse before they got better. Take monarchy, I said. It built up and up, grew more complex, more useless, more removed from government, in any real sense, until we come to things like England's Wars of the Roses and France's Sun King and the Czar and the Mikado—until most of the business of the government was in the person of the king, instead of the other way around. Then—bang! No more monarchy."

"Mr. President," whispered the voice in his ear, "you have an appointment with the Mongolian Legate."

"Oh, shut up, you," said the President amiably, shocking his prompter and confusing his guests. "Sorry, not you," he apologized. "My, uh, secretary. Tells me that the Chinese representatives want to talk about our 'unprecedented and unpeace-loving acts'—more likely, to see what they can find out." He picked the plug out of his ear and dropped it in a desk drawer. "They'll wait. Now, take slavery," he went on. "It too became more institutionalized—and ritualized— until the horse was riding the man; until the South here was existing on slaves, it was even existing *for* slaves. The biggest single item of wealth in the thirteen Confederate states was slaves. The biggest single line of business, other than agriculture, was slavery, dealing and breeding. Things get big and formal, you see, just before they pop and blow away. Well, I wrote all this up. I turned it in, real proud, expecting, I don't know, maybe an honorary LL.D. At least a compliment, certainly . . . It came back and the instructor had scrawled one word across the top of it: *Toynbee.* So I read up on Toynbee's books. After, of course, I got over being oppressed at the instructor's injustice to me. He was right. Toynbee described the whole thing long before I did.

"But, you know, I didn't know that at the time. I thought it up myself, as if Toynbee had never lived," said the President with some pride. He beamed at them.

Senator Horton was standing with open mouth. He glanced quickly at the others in the room, but they had nothing but puzzlement to return to him. He said, "Mr. President, I don't understand. You mean—"

"Mean? I mean what's happened to us," said the President testily. "We've had our obsessive period. Now we move on to something else. And, Senator, Congress is going to have to help move; and, I'm warning you, you're going to help me move *it.*"

When they left the White House it was late afternoon. The lilacs that bordered the wall were in full, fragrant bloom. Denzer inhaled deeply and squeezed the hand of Maggie Frome.

Passing the sentry box at the end of the drive, they heard a voice from a portable radio inside. It was screaming:

"It's going . . . it's *going* . . . it's GONE, folks! Craffany has pulled one out of the fire again! And that wraps it up for him, as Hockins sends one *way* out over centerfield and into the stands . . ." The guard looked out, rosily beaming, and waved them on. He would have waved them on if they had worn beards and carried ticking bombs; he was a Craffany rooter from way back, and now in an ecstasy of delight.

"Craffany did it, then," said Walter Chase sagely.

"I *thought* when he benched Hockins and moved Little Joe Fliederwick to—"

"Oh, shut up, Chase." said Denzer. "Maggie, I'm buying drinks. You want to come along, Venezuela?"

"I think not, Mr. Denzer," said the research man. "I'm late now. *Statist. Analysis Trans.* is expecting me."

"Chase?" Politeness forced that one out of him. But Chase shook his head.

"I just remembered an old friend here in town," said Chase. He had had time for some quick thinking. If the nation was going over to a non-shelter philosophy—if cave-dwelling was at an end and a dynamic new program was going to start—maybe a cement degree wasn't going to be the passport to security and fame he had imagined. Walter Chase had always had a keen eye for the handwriting on the wall. "A young lady friend," he winked. "Name of Douglasina Baggett. Perhaps you've heard of her father; he's quite an important man in H. E. and W."

The neutron, properly placed, had struck the nucleus; and the spreading chain was propagating rapidly through their world. What was it going to be from now on? They did not know; does a fissioned atom know what elements it will change into? It *must* change; and so it changes. "I guess we did something, eh?" said Denzer. "But . . . I don't know. If it hadn't been us, I expect it would have been someone else. Something had to give." For it doesn't matter which nucleus fissions first. Once the mass is critical the chain reaction begins; it is as simple as that.

"Let's get that drink, Denzer," said Maggie Frome.

They flagged a cab, and all the way out to Arlington-Alex it chuckled at them as they kissed. The cab spared them its canned thoughts, and that was as they wished it. But that was not why they were in each other's arms.

AFTERWORD

Some person who is not me will have to decide how great a writer Cyril Kornbluth was. I was too close to him, as collaborator in many ways, and as friend.

In all, we wrote four science-fiction novels together*, plus three novels which were not science fiction and, in various permutations, with and without other collaborators, several dozen stories.

There are still in my files a few fragments of stories, and one huge chunk of a novel, not science fiction, about the Civil War. For technical reasons I do not think the novel is likely ever to be finished and published by anybody. None of the other fragments have enough in them to go on, and so unless some unexpected treasure trove turns up there will be no more.

So I think that this volume, which contains stories published as long as a decade and a half after his death, contains the last of the work of Cyril Kornbluth which is ever likely to see print; and I regret very much the loss to all of us, and personally and particularly to myself, of this bright and rewarding talent.

*There was a fifth, *Marschild*, which began as a short story of mine but was otherwise written almost entirely by Cyril and my then wife, Judith Merril.

ABOUT THE AUTHORS

FREDERIK POHL has been called (by Kingsley Amis, in *New Maps of Hell*) "the most consistently able writer science fiction, in its modern form, has yet produced." He has won four Hugos, and is the only person ever to have won this coveted science fiction award both as editor and as writer. His work includes not only science fiction, in which he is an acknowledged master, but work as disparate as feature articles for *Playboy* and *Family Circle* and scholarly treatises, such as his biography of the Roman emperor Tiberius in the Encyclopaedia Britannica. In addition, he has lectured in Russia and at some two hundred and fifty colleges and has appeared on more than four hundred radio and television programs. He was recently President of the Science Fiction Writers of America, and is the author (with C. M. Kornbluth) of *The Space Merchants*, recognized as one of the all-time classics of science fiction. He is presently science fiction editor at Bantam Books, and makes his home in Red Bank, New Jersey.

CYRIL KORNBLUTH began writing science fiction for publication at the age of fifteen, and kept it up until his sadly early death in his mid-thirties. In his own right he was the author of four science fiction novels, including *The Syndic*, a number of works outside the science-fiction field and several score of the brightest and most innovative shorter science-fiction pieces ever written. Some of his short stories and novelettes have been mainstays for the anthologists ever since and have been adapted for television production, as for example *The Little Black Bag* and *The Marching Morons*. His collaboration with Frederik Pohl has been described as "the finest sf collaborating team in history." Together they wrote seven novels and more than thirty short stories, among their works such classics as *The Space Merchants*, which has been translated into more than thirty-five languages and has appeared on most lists of the most important science fiction novels ever written.